# LILY AND THE LION

A SCIFI ALIEN ROMANCE
(ALIEN ABDUCTION BOOK 12)

HONEY PHILLIPS

Copyright © 2021 by Honey Phillips

All rights reserved. No part of this book may be used or reproduced by any means, graphic, electronic, or mechanical, including photocopying, recording, taping or by any information storage retrieval system without the written permission of the author.

Disclaimer

This book is a work of fiction. Names, characters, places, and incidents are products of the author's imagination or are used fictitiously and are not to be construed as real. Any resemblance to actual events, locales, organizations, or people, living or dead, is entirely coincidental.

Cover by Maria Spada Book Cover Design
Edited by Lindsay York at LY Publishing Services

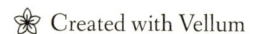

❀ Created with Vellum

CHAPTER ONE

"Fuck!" Lily screamed as the escape pod rocketed towards a planet far below. She had been shoved into the pod with no explanation by one of the alien bastards who had kidnapped her. In her attempt to resist, she had managed to land a solid kick to his balls before he was able to restrain her legs. He had responded by slapping her across the face. Her cheekbone still throbbed, but it wasn't the first time she'd been hit. She'd survive the blow.

Whether or not she was going to survive this descent was an entirely different matter. The air inside the pod kept getting hotter, and she could hear a terrifying rattle that reminded her of the sound her old car used to make just before it broke down. Periodically the pod would hitch a little, as if it was trying to slow, but it never seemed to have any effect.

Through the small porthole, she glimpsed the rapidly approaching planet—wide expanses of ocean and what looked like heavily forested land masses. She didn't see any signs of civilization—no cities or roads or farms. *Maybe that was a good thing*, she thought grimly. She'd rather take the chance of surviving on her own than being in the clutches of more aliens.

The land grew closer with dizzying speed, and she braced for impact just as the pod crashed into the trees. She could hear branches breaking beneath her, barely slowing the fall of the pod, but as they grew thicker, the shock of hitting each branch reverberated through the interior until it finally slammed into the ground with stunning force. The pod came to a halt, one side cracking open like an egg.

For a long time, she was too dazed to do anything but stare up at the broken branches and torn leaves above her. The faintly pinkish sky seemed to be a long way away above her, and some distant part of her mind wondered about the size of the trees. The leaves were an odd color as well—green with a slightly reddish tinge.

How did I end up here?

Only a few short weeks ago, she'd thought she might finally have found a place where she wanted to put down some roots. She had been living in the small town of Cosmo Beach for six months, and she liked it. The bar she managed catered to a predominantly local crowd, and even the occasional influx of tourists wasn't too disruptive. The small apartment above the bar that came with the job was nothing fancy, but it had windows that looked out over the ocean and it was all hers.

But then she discovered that Dave, her bartender and occasional lover, was stealing from the till. When she went to confront him, she'd found him in bed with a waitress she'd considered a friend. The woman's betrayal hurt much more than his theft.

After firing him, she wandered down to the beach. In all her years of traveling, she'd never lived by the ocean before, but she'd rapidly grown addicted to the sound of the waves and the vast expanse of water, the moon lighting a path to the distant horizon. She was only twenty-six, but she felt old tonight, old and alone. Sometimes it seemed like she spent her whole life running.

She'd left home at sixteen, chasing after Stryker, the improbably named lead singer in a local band. His declarations of undying love hadn't even lasted six months. She'd genuinely believed that she loved him—and that he loved her. His rejection devastated her, but then his older brother Barry, who managed the band, had taken her under his wing. He offered to let her stay with him, and he didn't ask anything from her. When she asked him to kiss her, she was convinced that it was her idea. She was with him for almost three years, and it wasn't until several years after they separated that she realized how easily he had manipulated her.

Barry had left the band after one of his periodic arguments with his brother escalated—and he hadn't asked her to come with him. At the time, she thought that perhaps their relationship had come to a natural conclusion, but looking back on it afterwards, she sometimes wondered if she had simply become too old for his tastes.

Lily had ended up stepping into his role in managing the band. That had lasted another three years—a slurred landscape of late nights and constant travel, too much alcohol and the wrong kind of men.

After her experiences with Stryker and Barry, she did her best to avoid entanglements, but life on the road had an odd kind of reality. And then one morning she woke up in yet another strange hotel room and realized she had no idea where she was. She didn't remember what city they were in—she didn't even know the date. Half a dozen strangers were passed out around the room, and the only person she recognized was Tony, the drummer, asleep in a chair by the window.

With a complete and utter certainty, she knew that this

wasn't what she wanted—she wasn't sure exactly what she did want, but she knew this wasn't it. She quietly gathered her small collection of belongings, then went over to Tony. He was a sweet man with long thinning grey hair who had been playing music since before she was born. She kissed his forehead, and he woke up and gave her a sleepy smile.

"What's up, baby girl?"

"I'm leaving."

He nodded thoughtfully. "It's probably time. But I'm going to miss you."

"I'll miss you too," she said sincerely. He had always done his best to look after her in his own lowkey way. She was willing to bet that he'd spent the night in the chair just in case things got out of hand.

Despite the band's nomadic lifestyle, she'd managed to put some money aside. She could have gone back to school, or tried to do something different with her life. Instead, she drifted into a job as a bartender. Since then she'd had a variety of jobs, but she never ended up staying anywhere longer than six or seven months. Even though she enjoyed most of her jobs, there had always been something to drive her on. A manager with roaming hands or another disastrous relationship or simply the restlessness that prodded her to keep moving. Cosmo Beach had been the first time she'd actually thought of sticking around.

Apparently, the gods had other plans for her.

She'd been sitting quietly on the beach that night when she caught a whiff of something horrible, followed by a sharp pinch to her neck. When she regained consciousness, she was in a small cage next to two other caged women, with an unfamiliar male leering at her.

An alien male. She had been abducted by fucking aliens. The translator they had placed in her ear meant that it was all too easy to understand their intentions. They planned to sell all three of them as sex slaves—and even though she had every intention of fighting, she knew that the odds were against her.

They had been confined to their cages for about two weeks—long enough to form an unbreakable bond between the three women. Kate was a scientist, cool, practical, and smart. Lily admired her intelligence and her determination to find a logical solution to their situations. Mary was quite different, innocent and optimistic. She'd even managed to point out positive aspects about their captors, and Lily believed she genuinely meant them. Of course, she was also the only one who received additional treats and soft words from the despicable bastards.

What happened to them? she wondered now, looking up at the sky. Earlier that day, Eshak, one of the most brutal aliens, had appeared and dragged Kate away without a word.

"What if we never see her again?" Mary had whispered, her eyes wide and frightened.

"We will," Lily said fiercely, determined to hide her own fears.

But then Eshak had returned for her, and she'd been forced to leave Mary behind. *Why?* Why had he dragged her into the pod, and why had they sent her to this planet?

She did her best to emulate Kate's cool logic. It seemed probable that all three of them had been forced into the pods—which meant that her friends could also be somewhere here in the jungle. She had to find them.

She allowed herself a few more moments to recover from the descent, but she refused to give into the dizziness for long. If she'd understood Eshak's muttered comments correctly, the slavers planned to recover their prizes. She didn't know how hard it would be for them to find the pod in this immense jungle, but the farther away she was from it, the better.

After wrestling with the restraints across her body, she

managed to release them and wiggle free. Very cautiously, she poked her head up through the open side of the pod—and discovered she hadn't hit the ground after all. The pod was wedged in the crevice between the branch that had stopped its fall and the huge tree trunk supporting the branch. *Great.* That meant she was going to have to climb down—and she had never been particularly good with heights.

She wiggled her way through the opening, tearing the wretched slave gown in the process. She would have loved to just throw it away, but the thought of being naked in the jungle wasn't much more appealing. In the end, she ripped the two pieces of white fabric apart. She twisted one piece into a crude bandeau bra and tied the other one around her hips to form a short sarong. Not quite the latest fashion, but at least it was her choice, not something forced on her by the alien slavers.

The climb down to the ground was nerve-wracking at best, despite the fact that the bark of the tree was heavily ridged and provided multiple hand and foot holds. Thank goodness she had been enough of a tomboy in her misspent youth to know how to climb—and that the pod hadn't crashed too far above the ground. She managed to avoid looking down, but her heart was still pounding when she jumped the last few feet and landed in the loam beneath the trees.

Now what?

CHAPTER TWO

Leotra va Situni walked into his spacious bedroom and came to an abrupt halt. A cloying perfume filled the air, not one that he would have ever chosen. His eyes went immediately to the bed, and sure enough, ripe female curves were clearly visible beneath the thin silk sheet.

He deliberately cleared his throat, and the female sat up, letting the sheet drift down to reveal the smooth pelt covering her obviously enhanced breasts. The work had been well done, accentuating her naturally sleek physique, and he felt a flicker of interest. But then he looked at her face and saw the avaricious gleam she couldn't quite hide behind her seductive façade.

"Out," he ordered.

White fangs flashed as she snarled, but then she crawled towards him, her tail twitching seductively. "But Leotra, it's been such a long time."

She knew him? Most of the women who showed up in his bed or his houses or his vehicles tended to be complete strangers. He took a second look at her face. Ah yes. She'd had work done there as well, but now he recognized her. Jinga. They'd had a brief and not particularly enjoyable liaison some years ago when he first came to maturity and was busy reaping the rewards of being heir to an extraordinarily rich and successful merchant house.

"I'm not interested, Jinga," he said firmly.

She paid absolutely no attention, slinking over to him and rubbing her body against his front while her tail tried to tangle with his. This close, he could catch the betraying hint of an artificial mating hormone, but he felt absolutely nothing, a reaction that was becoming all too common. The thought that he might be losing any sexual interest in the opposite sex horrified him, but not enough to try and reawaken it with this female.

Reaching behind him, he slapped a hand on the alert panel. Less than three seconds later, two enormous Bukharan guards burst into the room. Both of them were too well trained to reveal their shock that the alert was nothing more than an attractive naked female. They had seen many of them in his rooms over the years.

"Please remove Mistress Jinga. Find her some clothing and send her back to Yangu."

She snarled and sank her claws into the arm she had been stroking seductively. He refused to flinch, removing her hand as gently as possible. No matter how conniving she might be, he drew the line at hurting a female.

When Gorik clamped his hand on her shoulder, a lot less gently, and drew her back against his body, Leotra shook his head. "You are not permitted to damage her."

"Yes, sir."

He watched in disgust as the treacherous female immediately rubbed her hips against the guard. "My, you're so... big." She shot Leotra a challenging look. "Unlike some males I could mention."

He almost laughed. The last thing he was concerned about was her insulting his cock.

"Take her away."

Gorik hauled her out of the room, but Leotra noticed that he didn't attempt to push her away.

"Sir," Katta lingered. "Gorik is young and impulsive, but I wished to clarify your command..."

"I said no damage," he repeated firmly, then shrugged. "Willing consent is completely different—but Katta, I do mean willing."

"Yes, sir." A smile crossed Katta's face as he bowed and left.

He was not concerned that the male would disobey. His guards were chosen for their discipline and sense of honor, and they would not force a female. He wondered if Jinga knew what she was getting into, taking on two of the huge horned males.

No doubt she had employed a similar tactic to gain access to his rooms. Tomorrow, he would summon Hudomo and make it crystal clear that if it happened again, he would no longer retain his position as steward of his hunting lodge. Tonight, he didn't want to deal with it.

Crossing to the windows that led out onto the balcony, he flung them open, replacing the cool, overly perfumed air with the humid warmth of the jungle. The hunting lodge was a complex of buildings perched amongst the trees. From the outside, they appeared to be rustic if somewhat large shelters, but inside they contained every amenity. Unfortunately, the luxury came at the cost of a connection to the natural surroundings.

He crossed to the railing, breathing in the night scents and listening to the sounds of the jungle. His tail lashed restlessly. Whatever had driven him from the active social scene and hedonistic delights of his home planet of Yangu still haunted him.

The plan had been to take a hunting expedition into the jungle. There would be beaters to stir up the game, porters to carry everything necessary to set up an extravagant camp each night, his chef, his steward, and a number of other household staff. Right now, the thought only made him cringe.

Suddenly decisive, he returned to his room, stripping off the long, embroidered robe and the flowing silk pants. He searched through his wardrobe until he found an old leather loincloth, one he had used long ago when he was first learning the ways of the jungle. He tied it around his waist and added his favorite hunting knife, already feeling less restricted. Leaving a brief message to be delivered to Hudomo in the morning, he returned to the balcony. The nearest limb was no more than ten feet away. He leapt easily across the distance, his claws sinking into the soft bark.

An exhilarated roar rose in his chest but he forced it back. It would only alert his household. Instead, he began moving easily through the trees. By the time they received his message, he would be miles away.

Lily studied the area beneath the huge tree, her heart sinking. The only thing she could see was more of the massive trees, interspersed with smaller trees and some low bushes with spiky orange leaves. She'd never been much of a nature lover, but nothing around her looked the slightest bit familiar. Instead of the greens and browns she would have expected, the colors were much more vibrant. The leaves were tinged with deep reds and oranges. She could hear rustling in the undergrowth, along with the constant whirr of what she assumed were insects, occasionally interspersed with a distant cry that made her shiver.

Down here on the ground there was no trace of the crash, and for a moment despair overwhelmed her. Even if one of her friends had fallen nearby, she could walk beneath the crash site without ever knowing that it was there. *No*, she refused to think like that. Kate would be sure and find a way out of the pod, and she didn't think that Mary was just going to sit around and wait for the slavers to return. They would break free just as she had. *If they're alive*, her pessimistic side prompted, but she refused to accept that possibility.

If she couldn't find any sign of them on the ground, she would need to get higher. The thought of climbing one of the humongous trees made her shiver, but it seemed like the only alternative. But not here. She still needed to get as far away from this place as she could first.

Turning in a slow circle, she tried to decide on a direction. Everything looked identical until she caught a faint glimpse of something shimmering in the distance. Water perhaps?

The thought made her realize just how thirsty she felt, so with a mental shrug, she headed in that direction. She tried to keep track of her path, but everything looked so similar. *I really should have stayed in the Girl Scouts*. Instead, she'd been kicked out for smoking on an overnight camping trip. She tried to remember if she'd learned anything useful before then.

Wasn't there something about where moss grew on trees? She took a closer look at her surroundings and decided there was something—not moss exactly—that seemed to appear consistently on one side of the largest trees. Triumphant about her discovery, she walked with renewed confidence.

The sounds of the jungle had a disturbing tendency to fade away as she approached and resume once she passed by, but she finally decided that was a positive thing. Maybe whatever was making those noises was as scared of her as she was scared of it. Then a harsh growl sounded from the branches directly overhead, and her heart skipped a beat. She froze for a terrified moment before diving into the underbrush at the base of the nearest tree. *Of course the slave gown had to be white*, she thought bitterly as she tried to blend in to the vibrant leaves. Of course her skin wasn't a lot darker. Only her red hair might provide some type of camouflage.

Crouched amongst the bushes, her heart pounding, she searched for some type of weapon. The only thing she could spot was a hefty branch a short distance away. She dragged it towards her as quietly as possible, listening for any other signs of what she was sure was a predator. The normal sounds of the jungle started up around her again, and she took a deep breath. *Fuck it.* She'd never been the type to cower in a corner, and she wasn't about to start now. Taking a firmer grip on her branch, she stepped cautiously out of the bushes. She looked up, searching for any sign of the animal that had growled so loudly, but she could see nothing except leaves and branches. It appeared to have moved on.

Still clutching the branch, she resumed her journey towards the sparkle of light in the distance. She did her best to keep her eyes and ears open, but the rest of the walk passed without incident before she emerged in a small clearing at the edge of a good-sized river.

The sunlight played across the surface, the water a slightly purplish blue, reminding her that she was a long way from home. Was it even water? Her mouth and throat were painfully dry, but she hovered indecisively on the bank for several minutes before she decided to dip the end of her branch into the swiftly running liquid. Pulling it free, she put a hesitant fingertip to the damp surface. It felt like water. She sniffed her fingertip but couldn't detect anything unusual. Finally, she put her tongue to the damp surface. It tasted, well, like water.

She shrugged again. She couldn't survive without water so she didn't really have a choice. Crouching down, she leaned forward to dip her hand in the water—and a big body slammed into her, knocking her away from the river.

She had a brief impression of soft fur and tremendous strength and then it was gone. She scrabbled backwards, knocking her head against the base of a tree with a painful thunk. Her head pounding, she searched frantically for whatever had attacked her. Her mouth went dry at the sight of a strange alien crouched at the other side of the clearing.

But this alien was nothing like the ones on the ship. They had been short, stocky, and hairy, rather like cavemen. The male looking at her now was huge, with short golden fur covering his impressively muscled body. A wild mane in every shade of gold and brown surrounded a face that was not entirely alien but was most definitely not human. There was a distinctly feline aspect to his features, with a wide, flat nose and an equally wide mouth with prominently displayed white fangs. His eyes were a startlingly intense blue with vertical cat-like pupils, and they stared at her hungrily.

Was he like a cat? Was he playing with his prey? She suddenly remembered the stray cat that haunted the back of the bar, and a hysterical giggle threatened to emerge.

"Nice kitty," she whispered instead. "You're a nice kitty, aren't you? You don't want to eat me, do you?"

Something flickered across his expression, too fast for her to read, and then he prowled towards her.

CHAPTER THREE

Leotra heard the female give a startled gasp as he approached, but he kept going. When he had first seen her, cautiously moving through the jungle, his first impulse had been anger. A female had even managed to find him here? But then she had fled into the underbrush at the sound of his growl, long legs flashing, and the sight had startled him enough to break through his anger.

He didn't see how it would be possible for anyone to know his location. On the other hand, he'd had females "accidentally" appear in stranger places. Although his first impulse had been to confront her and demand an explanation, in the end he had decided to keep watch instead.

When she emerged from her hiding place, a branch gripped in one small fist and a defiant look on her face, he'd been intrigued. He didn't recognize the species, but it was certainly an attractive one. Long legs, softly curved hips, and high, full breasts, all invitingly displayed in a skimpy white outfit. Her clothing seemed designed to lure rather than to protect her from the hazards of the jungle—he could see faint red marks on her delicate skin from her sojourn in the bushes—which argued that his original suspicion was correct. Her walk too was remarkably seductive, even without the swing of a tail to accentuate the gentle sway of those lush hips.

But she didn't seem to be searching for him. Instead, she was moving in a remarkably straight line for someone who was obviously new to the jungle. He frowned when he realized she was heading for the river. Did she realize how dangerous that would be? Or perhaps she was meeting someone there—the rivers were navigable with an experienced captain. He was still turning over the possibilities of who might have succumbed to her advances and brought her here when she reached the riverbank. No boats were in sight, and he watched curiously as she probed the water with her stick. Then, to his horror, she bent down towards the water.

He managed to knock her out of the way before a namba could emerge, but that one moment of feeling her soft, silky body beneath him made his cock stiffen. He'd remained crouched in order to hide his erection, watching with a mixture of dismay and amusement she tried to scramble away from him. Didn't she realize he was the least of her worries?

Her eyes had widened at the sight of him, and he had waited for the usual seductive smile or reverent gaze.

But either she didn't recognize him or she was playing some other game. Then his implant translated her words. *Kitty?* The translation wasn't exact but she apparently thought he was some kind of animal. And a small one at that.

Outraged, and determined to teach her a lesson, he prowled over to her. If she expected an animal, he'd show her an animal. He bent over her bare leg, sniffing loudly at the exposed flesh and gradually working his way up from her ankle. Mmm. She smelled delightful. He breathed in more of her delicious scent as he reached her thighs and unable to resist, he swiped his tongue across the pale silky flesh. He heard her gasp, but he was too intrigued by his new toy to pay much attention. He moved higher, to the source of that tantalizing fragrance, but just as he started to work his way under the scrap of white fabric, a branch slammed into the side of his head.

He rolled aside, more shocked than hurt, as she tried to climb to her feet. *Oh no.* She wasn't getting away from him that easily. He dove at her again, and this time he didn't let her go.

She fought wildly, her small fists pounding on his shoulders as she writhed beneath them. But even though she managed to get in a few surprisingly painful blows, he was too distracted by the feel of all that soft flesh rubbing against him to really care. He finally used more of his weight to keep her in place, and his aching shaft came to rest against her soft stomach. He growled softly in her ear, and she froze.

"Nice kitty," she said breathlessly. "Please be a nice kitty."

The insult didn't seem as important when her scent surrounded him and he could feel the hard points of her nipples against his chest. He drew in another breath. He could detect a hint of fear but there was a deeper note that spoke of her arousal. Was she truly afraid? Or was this part of a bigger trap, designed to appeal to his hunting instinct?

Part of him wanted to demand answers, but the rest was still suspicious as to her motives. If she really thought he was no more than an animal, he would go along with it. For now.

She tried to wiggle out from beneath him again, and the movement made his cock jerk. Apparently, he didn't need to worry about his lack of sexual interest. All he needed was to tackle a half-naked female in the jungle. But this was not the time to explore that interest. He growled in her ear again, and once again she froze.

As delightful as it was to feel her pinned beneath him, he wouldn't get any answers this way. He lifted his upper body enough to be able to look down at her. A wild tangle of red hair spread around her on the ground, the colors as rich as the kani leaves. The rest of her skin was smooth and hairless, as defenseless as it had appeared when he watched her, delightfully soft against his fur. Her features were small and delicate with a pointed little nose and a tiny, lush mouth. *Her mouth would be far too small to take my cock,* he thought regretfully, even though his cock jerked again at the image. Her eyes widened, as blue as his own despite their odd shape, and he knew she had felt him respond. A small pink tongue licked nervously at her lips, and he had the oddest desire to stroke it with his own.

But then her eyes narrowed and her expression turned fierce. "Get off me, you big oaf."

She bucked up against him as she spoke but all that did was thrust her lower body more closely against his aching cock. She gave a frustrated growl of her own, and he sighed. As much as he was enjoying this game, and even though he was sure she was aroused, she didn't seem to want to play. He reluctantly climbed off of her.

He half-expected her to plunge into the trees, but although she backed away from him, she only went far enough to grab hold of her stick. That must have been what she hit him with before. He almost laughed. If it hadn't worked the first time, why would she think it would work now? Still, he admired her courage.

Giving her time to decide on her next move, he rose to his feet and went to collect one of the large kani leaves from the base of the tree. He deliberately turned his back on her, but she didn't attack. She also didn't run away, and once again he wondered about her motives. When he turned back towards her, she was studying him thoughtfully.

"You're wearing clothes," she said finally and he did his

best to hide his outrage. She really did think he was an animal, didn't she?

"I don't suppose you speak English? Or that you understand what I'm saying?"

Should he let her know that he understood? Or should he wait and see if she would divulge her real reason for being here?

"Umm, I came from the sky." She actually pointed into the air and he did his best not to roll his eyes. Even the most primitive male would surely realize she was not a native to their world. But then again, it might be helpful to establish a base level of conversation.

"Sky," he repeated, mimicking her gesture.

She nodded excitedly, which made her breasts jiggle in the most delightful way. He was so focused on the quivering flesh that he almost missed her next words.

"I had two friends in the sky." She waved two fingers at him. "I'm trying to find them. Have you seen anyone else like me?"

Two friends? What kind of friends? He didn't mind the thought of other females, but the thought that she might be searching for male friends almost made him growl. She was *his* toy. He wanted to demand answers, but he still wasn't ready to reveal how much he understood. Instead, he held up two fingers of his own.

She bobbed her head enthusiastically, her breasts bouncing again—which truly was most distracting.

"Have you seen them?" She actually took a step towards him, but he only gave her a blank stare. Her shoulder sagged, and he had an unexpected impulse to reassure her, but he had seen no other sign of strangers in his jungle.

"What about a village? Do you live with other people? In houses?"

Using her stick, she sketched a crude outline of what he assumed was supposed to be a house on the ground, followed by another. She really wasn't very good at this, but she was determined.

He reached for her stick, but she took a step back and glared at him. Shrugging, he used his claws instead to sketch a single building. When he looked up at her, she was staring at his hand in horrified fascination. It took him a minute to realize that she had no claws of her own. Poor, defenseless little female. *Well, perhaps not entirely defenseless,* he thought, ruefully rubbing the spot when she had hit him with her stick.

"Umm, I'm sorry about that, but you should keep your nose where it belongs."

He sat back on his heels and looked up at her. Given the difference between their height, the scrap of white fabric that barely covered her cunt was directly in front of him. All he would have to do was lean forward and pull her against his face...

She must have read something in his expression because she took a hasty step back.

"Only one house? There must be more of you somewhere. I guess a telephone is too much to hope for," she babbled as he hid a smile. "But maybe you at least have some food and some water?"

She cast a longing glance towards the water, reminding him of what he'd been doing. He found the kani leaf and used it to dip out some water and bring it to her. She drank thirstily, and he found it oddly satisfying. He couldn't remember the last time he'd served someone else. When he tried to offer her a second leaf full, she shook her head.

"I think I'd better wait and see if this upsets my system or not." She looked out at the river, then back at him. "Why didn't you let me get water for myself?"

He reached out his hand for her stick again, waiting patiently. A surge of satisfaction went through him when she sighed and reluctantly passed it over to him. He dangled the end of the stick in the water, making a small circle.

"What are you—oh my God!" She gave a horrified gasp as a namba emerged from the water and seized the stick in its enormous jaws. He released it immediately, and the namba disappeared beneath the water with its prize.

"What was that?" she asked shakily.

"Namba."

"I had no idea." She shuddered, then smiled at him. "I guess that explains why you tackled me. Thank you... Leo."

His hackles immediately went up as his previous suspicions flared. How did she know his name? Or at least a form of it?

"You don't mind if I call you that, do you?" she added. "Leo is the sign of the lion."

He wasn't sure that the words translated correctly—or that her explanation was truthful—but he shrugged, and pointed to her.

"Me? My name is Lily. It's a kind of flower."

No wonder she smelled so delightful. A most appropriate name.

"Lily," he repeated.

"That's right." She smiled at him, then looked up at the sky. "I think it's starting to get dark. Maybe we should go to your house? Then we can figure out where to go from there."

He wasn't about to take her back to his hunting lodge, at least not yet. But she was right—they didn't need to be in the open when night fell. He would find an appropriate place for them to shelter on a temporary basis, then see what other information he could discover from her.

CHAPTER FOUR

Lily followed the big lion alien through the jungle, still not entirely sure she was doing the right thing. But the sight of that monstrous mouth emerging from the river had been a fairly significant sign that she needed help. As much as she preferred to rely on herself, she didn't know the ways of the jungle.

And he seemed... well, certainly not harmless. Perhaps well-intentioned was a better word. She was quite sure that he had knocked her down in order to prevent her from being foolish enough to put her hand in the water. She could even explain away his sniffing his way up her body as his way of identifying her. At first, she'd been too paralyzed to respond, but then he'd licked her inner thigh. And even though that big, rough tongue had felt surprisingly—disturbingly—good it had shocked her back into awareness just as he started to push aside her skirt.

Unfortunately, hitting him with her branch had only resulted in him pinning her to the ground. But even though he had been obviously aroused, he hadn't made any attempt to take it further. Her nipples pebbled at the memory of that huge muscled body—and equally massive cock—pressing into her. *Don't be ridiculous,* she scolded herself. Just because she'd always had a thing for big men didn't mean it translated to an alien male. *It was just a physical reaction.*

But she still found herself watching him, the muscles in his broad back moving easily, his tail flicking back and forth. *A tail!* Surely that should be enough to discourage her lustful thoughts, but instead it only seemed to draw her attention to that round, firm ass barely covered by the small loincloth.

The loincloth had been what had convinced her to try talking to him. She'd hoped that it indicated some type of civilization. Not that she was expecting much, but if there was one alien, there had to be others, and perhaps one of them would know something about her friends. Although she would have felt a little more confident if he had drawn more than one building.

But he must have come from somewhere, she thought. And he must have had parents at some point. Hopefully he wasn't as estranged from them as she was from hers. She called them once, when Stryker dumped her, but they'd told her she had to live with her mistake. They hadn't wanted her back. The memory of that still stung, even all these years later.

Pushing the memory aside with the ease of long practice, she concentrated on Leo, striding confidently through the jungle. It was definitely getting darker now, and she wondered how much further they had to go.

"Leo? Is it much farther?"

He stopped and turned back to her, his eyes reflecting the light like a cat's eyes. She wasn't quite sure how much he understood, but hopefully it was enough. It would have been nice if he'd had one of those weird translator things the slavers had shoved in her ear.

"How far?" she repeated, using her fingers to mimic a walking motion. His fangs flashed white, and her heart skipped a beat before she realized he was smiling. She put her hands on her hips and huffed at him. "It's not my fault you don't speak English."

Even in the dim light, she could see his expression change. His eyes dropped to her breasts, and she realized her pose had thrust them out. It certainly wasn't the first time that she experienced that type of lustful look, but coming from a big feline alien in the growing darkness of the jungle it felt different. More primitive, more primal. Something inside her quivered in response.

He took two steps towards her, then bent his head and sniffed her neck, growling softly. The low reverberation sent a shiver down her spine and left a deep ache between her legs.

It's the jungle, she told herself quickly, and took a step back, even though part of her wanted to feel the press of those fur covered muscles against her skin once more.

"How much farther?" she repeated, her voice unexpectedly husky.

Instead of responding, he bent down and threw her over his shoulder. Oh my God. This wasn't how she envisioned touching him. Before she could try and wiggle free, he leapt into the air and landed on the trunk of one of the enormous trees. Even though one arm was locked securely around her legs, holding them against his chest, he began to climb. With her head dangling down his back, she could see the ground disappearing below them.

An embarrassingly girlish squeak escaped from her lips as she grabbed at him. One hand clutched the belt holding his loincloth in place while her other hand ended up on his tail. She squeezed it as he seemed to falter for a heart-stopping moment, but then he resumed the climb, moving even quicker.

Closing her eyes, she kept a tight grip on her hand holds and waited for him to reach whatever destination he had in mind.

When he finally came to a halt, it took her a moment to realize that he was standing as easily as if he was on the ground. She cautiously opened an eye and saw a wide branch beneath them. It was broad enough to stand on, but she was still reluctant to relinquish her grip. It wasn't until he bent forward and put her feet on the branch that she finally let go. His tail slid through her hand, and she thought she heard him growl again, but she was too busy making sure she wasn't going to fall to worry about it.

The branch did feel sturdy, and it was easily three or four feet wide, but why had he carried her up here? Before she could ask, he moved past her to the main trunk of the tree. A dark hollow marked the place where the branch and the trunk joined, and she watched in increasing dismay as he brushed debris out of the hollow. She had a sinking feeling this was where they were going to spend the night.

Her suspicions proved correct. Once he was satisfied, he motioned for her to join him. She took a cautious step in his direction, then another, but couldn't quite make herself enter the dark space. He shook his head, and then she was flying through the air as he picked her up and gently deposited her in the hollow. Once inside, it wasn't as bad as she had feared. The surrounding wood was dry and had a faint, pleasant earthy scent. What appeared to be crumbled bark cradled her body as she suddenly realized just how tired and sore she felt.

Leo bent down over her.

"Stay," he said firmly, then disappeared into the increasing darkness.

She nodded absently as she wiggled her way into a more comfortable position, then froze. She hadn't used that word with him. If he knew even a few words of a language that the translator could interpret, didn't that mean he must have had contact with someone who spoke another language? A language that an interstellar translator could recognize.

Her heart started to beat faster. Maybe there was a way out of here after all. And a way to find her friends. She waited impatiently for him to return but despite her impatience, she found herself battling exhaustion. She had slept very little during the weeks on board the alien spaceship, always afraid that one of the guards would go beyond lecherous threats, and the exertion of the day after an extended period of inactivity had tired her out. She felt strangely safe here, tucked into this little hollow, and the thought of Leo returning only added to that feeling of safety. Despite her best efforts, her eyes had closed before he returned.

CHAPTER FIVE

Leotra dropped quietly down through the branches of the tree, seeking the prey that would emerge in the shadowed time between sunset and full dark. The animals of the day were getting ready to retreat to their burrows while the nighttime prowlers were just beginning to emerge from their dens. A flash of movement caught his attention, and he pounced on a small marsupial, biting deep into the neck for a quick kill. Some of his acquaintances, including his own father, like to draw out the kill, but he had never really seen the appeal of torturing a frightened animal.

Using his knife, he quickly skinned and cleaned his catch, wrapping the flesh in more of the kani leaves just before the light faded completely. His night sight was still more than adequate for him to find his way back to Lily, even without the soft shimmer from the many bioluminescent plants that festooned the trees. He paused on the way to draw some sap from a moni tree into another leaf. It would serve to keep them hydrated until they reached another source of water. They weren't far from a set of springs. He had originally intended to camp there tonight, but he had noticed that Lily's steps were faltering and decided she needed to rest.

He wasn't surprised when he returned to the hollow and found that she was asleep. He was tempted to let her remain asleep, but she needed to eat in order to keep up her strength. For a moment, guilt washed over him. Why was he keeping her out here? He should take her back to the lodge and all the comforts he could provide.

No. He needed to find out more about why she was here first. And... out here he had her all to himself. He liked that feeling, just as he liked knowing that he was the one providing for her. Not his staff or his credits or any of the resources he normally had at his disposal—just his teeth and his claws and his knowledge of the jungle.

He crouched down and ran a gentle finger down the silken curve of her cheek. Was all her skin that soft? Or were her breasts even softer? Or the hidden place between her legs?

Her eyelids fluttered open, and with his night vision he could see the deep blue of her eyes and the way her lips curved at the sight of him.

"Leo," she whispered. No one had ever used a shortened version of his name before, but it sounded perfect coming from those rosy lips.

He opened his mouth to tell her so, then caught himself. If he revealed how much he understood, he would be forced into having a conversation he did not yet wish to have.

"Food," he said instead.

He saw her eyes widen as she pushed herself upright.

"I knew it. You can speak words the translator recognizes. What language are you speaking? Do you know other people who come from space? From the sky?"

Even though he didn't think she could see him very well, he kept his face impassive.

"Food."

Her face fell, and the feeling of guilt resurfaced. It was not an emotion he enjoyed, so he did his best to push it aside as she crawled cautiously out of the hollow and looked around.

"Ooh, it's so pretty. Like little candles in the trees."

He suspected she would rather not know that the bioluminescence was specifically designed to trap the prey of the flowering plants.

As she crossed her legs and leaned back against the trunk, he could see a tantalizing little patch of red fur shielding her cunt and realized she must think herself safe in the darkness. But despite the accuracy of his night vision, he suddenly wished it was full daylight so he could see every perfect little detail. His mouth watered at the thought of exploring those delicate folds.

"Uh, Leo? Did you say something about food?"

The sound of her voice finally penetrated his lustful haze.

"Yes," he said, then winced. He was revealing more knowledge about his ability to speak and understand than he had intended.

"Yes?" She laughed. "That's a good word. Do you know *no* as well?"

Her tone was light, almost teasing, but somehow she managed to sound provocative as well and all of his suspicions came rushing back.

"Food." His voice came out rougher than he had intended as he thrust the leaf in her direction. *Fuck.* She had him completely off of his usual game.

She took the leaf but gave the slab of meat a dubious look. He wondered how much could she see in the dim red glow.

"I don't suppose you can tell me what this is?" She held up her hand before he could respond. "Please just don't say food."

"Tigal," he responded, unable to keep a smug note out of

his voice since he was certain the name of the animal would be meaningless to her.

She huffed, muttering under her breath. "Serves me right for asking."

Poking the slab of meat with one finger, she shuddered. "Oh, God. Please tell me this isn't just a raw steak."

She looked up at him as she spoke, and he noticed her small blunt teeth again. Guilt immediately washed over him. He'd been so proud of himself for hunting for her, but he hadn't taken into consideration her natural limitations. When he reached out to take the leaf back, she surprised him by trying to hang onto it.

"No, it's all right. I don't mean to complain—I know I need to eat something."

He pulled out his knife and she shrank back, but he could see her glaring at him.

"Fine. I don't think it's very nice to taunt a girl with food and then take it away again."

"Cut," he said, sighing. He was expanding his vocabulary much quicker than he wanted.

Before she could ask any more questions, he began slicing the tigal meat into paper thin strips. As soon as he was finished, he pushed the leaf back towards her. She gave him a suspicious look.

"For keeps this time?"

"Yes," he growled.

Despite her obvious desire for food, she still hesitated before picking up one of the thin slices, then popping it in her mouth. He could see the changing expressions play across her face, distaste followed by surprise followed by thoughtfulness.

"This is a lot better than I expected. I had steak tartare once when Barry was feeling generous and it's kind of like that." She took the second slice much more readily. "It could use a little salt, but it's really good."

Who was Barry, and why had he been feeding Leo's female? He found himself growling before the full impact of his thoughts struck him. She was not his female, and her past was irrelevant.

Her eyes had widened again when he growled. "Am I eating too much? Are we supposed to be sharing this?"

"No."

The worry disappeared from her expression, followed by a surprisingly provocative smile.

"So you know that word too. Which do you like better, Leo, yes or no?"

Under other circumstances he would have had a thousand witty, flirtatious remarks at his disposal but given his choice to limit his vocabulary, he didn't have many options. Instead, he leaned forward and stroked his finger across the exact spot on her inner thigh where he had licked her earlier.

"Yes," he growled, then sat back.

Her little pink tongue licked at her lips again, and her scent deepened, but then she lifted her chin and gave him a challenging look.

"I prefer no."

Clever female. Under other circumstances, he would have continued the game, but he preferred games where he knew everyone's motivation. He still was unsure of hers.

Instead, he picked up the carcass of the tigal and settled down to enjoy his own meal. Meat in its most basic form, fresh from the hunt, had fallen out of favor on Yangu. It was still a primary component of their diet, but it was sauced, spiced, smoked, and prepared in a thousand different subtle and enticing ways. He had forgotten the sheer pleasure of consuming his prey.

A hastily drawn breath made him look up to see Lily staring at him.

"I guess table manners aren't big in the jungle, are they?"

He nearly laughed. His etiquette teacher would have been equally appalled.

"But I guess it's not that much worse than seeing Dave attack a pile of barbecued ribs."

Despite her attempt to sound nonchalant, he noticed she kept her eyes averted, and he suddenly found himself annoyed. He didn't like her comparing him to another male, and he didn't like the fact that she found him so uncivilized. He couldn't wait to introduce her to the twenty pieces of required silverware in a formal Tajiri meal.

No. There would be no formal meal, and he wouldn't be introducing her to anything. As soon as he found out why she was here, he would send her back the way she had come. He was still trying to come up with some feasible explanation for her presence when she spoke again.

"That was very good. Thank you."

To his astonishment, she had consumed all of the meat and was patting her flat stomach with a lazy, satisfied expression. *Would she look like that after sex?* he wondered, and his shaft immediately responded. He sternly told it to behave—which had no visible effect—and reached for the moni sap.

"Drink."

"Ah, a new word. I wonder how many you actually know."

She sent him a challenging look, but he ignored it, simply holding out the cup-shaped leaf containing the moni sap until she took it from him. She took a sip, then smiled and took another.

"This is delicious. Almost like coconut milk." A yawn interrupted her words, and she gave him a sleepy smile. "I'm sorry. I haven't slept well in... a long time."

He couldn't resist. "Sleep."

She laughed, moving back into the hollow in the tree. "Just you wait. I'll have you up to fifteen words by tomorrow."

She curled up, put her head on her arm, and almost immediately her breathing turned slow and even. He watched her sleep, feeling unexpectedly content. He had provided for her, and now she slept under his protection. It was surprisingly rewarding.

Eventually, he tore himself away and cleaned up the remains of their meal, tossing the few remaining scraps to some of the hungry plants on an adjoining branch. He left the moni sap to ripen overnight, then crawled into the hollow with her. She stirred as he pulled her into his arms, but he made a soothing sound, his chest reverberating against her back, and she soon settled down again.

Sleep did not come as easily for him. The feel of her soft body nestled against him, her lush hips cradling the erection he was completely helpless to control, was almost unbearably tempting. The irony of the situation did not escape him. If he had remained in his lodge, he would have had no difficulty finding a female to satisfy him—but back at the lodge, he'd had no desire for a female.

Be careful what you wish for, his grandfather had always said and as usual, his grandfather had been right.

But still, nestled here in the embrace of the tree with his female in his arms, surrounded by the sounds and scents of the jungle, he couldn't regret the impulse that had driven him away from the lodge. Tomorrow, he would find out more about this mysterious female and if his suspicions proved to be correct... His fangs glinted in the soft glow of the flowers. He was going to have a lot of fun with her.

CHAPTER SIX

Lily woke up nestled against something big and furry. A low, rhythmic purr vibrated against her back, and for a confused moment she wondered if the cat she had been feeding had crawled into bed with her. But then a massive arm tightened around her stomach and it all came rushing back. Her abduction, the perilous descent to the planet, and the big lion-like alien male who had found her.

Considering the way he was wrapped around her, he seemed to think he had established a claim on her. Should she be worried about it? Probably not, she decided. In her experience, that initial possessiveness never lasted. But for right now, he had fed her and protected her and seemed to be taking her somewhere—hopefully somewhere more civilized. The trick would be keeping him interested enough to help her, but not so interested that he wanted to hide her away in the jungle forever.

Her feminine charms seemed to be enough to hold his interest so far. Then again, given the size of the erection currently prodding against her backside, maybe he didn't have a lot of experience with females. She was almost tempted to reach back and explore that thick length, but although he hadn't attempted to force himself on her yet, she didn't want to rouse the beast.

And it really did feel like a beast, she thought with a silent giggle and just the tiniest little experimental movement. The next thing she knew, she was flat on her back with Leo leaning down over her, blue eyes blazing. His broad shoulders completely blotted out the daylight seeping into the hollow, and her breath caught. She had forgotten just how big he was.

His mouth opened as if he was about to say something, but then he shut it again and shook his head, frustration clear on his face. His erection was wedged firmly between her legs and she felt a pulse of desire as he looked down at her. She followed his gaze and saw that her makeshift top had shifted during the night, exposing one of her breasts. Her nipple was taut, almost quivering from a strange combination of excitement and nerves. She wasn't exactly afraid, but this was completely outside of her experience—even if it wasn't the first time she had woken up with a virtual stranger in her bed.

But never an alien, she reminded herself, and almost laughed.

He tilted his head, still studying her, and the morning light caught glitters of gold in his wildly curling mane. Before she could second-guess herself, she reached up and wrapped a curl around her finger. She wasn't quite sure what she'd expected— something coarser perhaps—but it was as silky as her own hair although there was so much more of it. She combed her fingers deeper into the thick strands, and he leaned into her touch. She felt the same low reverberation she had felt earlier all along her body and realized he was purring. The sensation was almost like a full-body vibrator, and she had the urge to press closer.

His eyes had shut while she played with his mane, but they snapped open now, the hunger in his gaze clearly visible.

Maybe you shouldn't pet the big kitty, she told herself nervously, just as his head descended to her neck. He sniffed her there, breathing in her scent and sending a shiver across the sensitive nerve endings. And then he licked her, his tongue as warm and wet and rough as she remembered, and she almost moaned. Her neck had always been extraordinarily sensitive. His mouth trailed down her neck and across her chest, and she couldn't prevent herself from crying out as that wonderful tongue curved around her taut nipple. She started to arch into his touch before she came to her senses.

"No." She pushed against his shoulders, even though she had no chance of moving him unless he cooperated. To her vast relief, he lifted his head and looked down at her.

"No?" he asked.

He swiped his tongue across her distended rosy nipple again and she couldn't prevent herself from quivering at the erotic sight.

"Yes. I mean no. No nipple licking."

"Nipple," he said thoughtfully and flicked the taut bud with a thick finger.

"Yes, that's my nipple. No touching either."

He tilted his head again, then bent down and fastened his mouth around her nipple and sucked. Oh my God. She felt the pull all the way down to her throbbing clit.

"No sucking either," she managed to say, but even she didn't find her voice convincing.

Nonetheless, he raised his head. He studied her face—which she suspected was bright red by now—with a degree of smug satisfaction that helped her ignore her demanding body.

"And I think that's enough of the language lessons for this morning."

She pushed at his shoulders again, trying to ignore just how good those big fur-covered muscles felt, but he ignored her, still studying her face. Before she could ask him to move, he bent down and brushed his lips against hers.

"Kiss," he whispered against her mouth, and then he was gone.

Her body felt unexpectedly cold without that big heated presence on top of her, even though the air was as warm and humid as it had been the day before. *Don't be silly*, she scolded herself and sat up. Leo was already outside on the branch and she hastily re-fastened her bandeau and went to join him.

Now that the sun was up, she could easily see how high they were in the trees and her stomach did a little flip. Careful to avoid looking down again, she took the cup-shaped leaf he offered her. The liquid from the night before tasted even better this morning, creating a satisfying warmth in her stomach.

"This is almost as good as coffee," she told him with a smile, but then her lips trembled as the realization hit her. There would be no coffee in her future.

She'd never been hopelessly addicted to the beverage, but she'd always loved that first taste of coffee in the morning. Even if it was more likely to be watery hotel coffee or a cheap cup from the gas station than the rare splurge at Starbucks, it had always been a part of her life.

"I'm never going to have coffee again, am I?" she whispered.

The urge to cry made her eyes burn, but she had learned a long time ago that crying never really changed anything. She usually preferred to channel her sadness into anger. But then Leo stepped forward and put his arms around her, drawing her into the warmth of his body, and she couldn't help herself. Her pent-up emotions burst out in a flood of tears, and she sobbed into his chest.

The flood didn't last long, but she felt better when it was over, lighter somehow. She gave a last sniffle and scrubbed at her face with her hands before giving him a shaky smile.

"Sorry. I don't usually give in to my emotions like them, but it's been a rough few weeks." A rough few years actually.

He opened his mouth, then shook his head, looking frustrated again. She gave his chest a reassuring pat.

"I know. It's hard when you can't communicate."

His frustration turned to something that looked oddly like guilt, but it vanished so quickly she wasn't sure that she had seen it. And really, she shouldn't be expecting human expressions on an alien face. Even though she already felt as if she was beginning to understand him.

"What's the plan for today?" she asked. "Are we going to your house?"

He hesitated, then shook his head. *Fuck.* The tree had been more comfortable than she expected, but it would be really nice to spend the night in an actual bed. If he even had a bed, of course...

"Two." He held up two fingers.

"Do you mean two days? Two days to get to your house?"

He nodded, and she wondered once again what type of communication he'd had with people who spoke a language her translator could recognize.

"How do you know these words? Did someone teach you?"

For a moment she thought he wasn't going to answer, and then a wicked look crossed his face.

"Teach." He leaned closer and stroked his thumb across her nipple, leaving a trail of fire behind. "Nipple."

"I don't think you need any more of those lessons," she said, torn between the urge to see what else she could teach him and the desire to wipe the smug look off of his face.

He simply grinned at her, his fangs glinting in the morning

light. Then he bent down again, and she realized he was about to put her over his shoulder.

"Wait a minute," she said quickly, stepping back. "Isn't there another way you could carry me?"

He raised an eyebrow in an oddly human gesture.

"Maybe I could get on your back instead?"

He tilted his head, then shrugged and turned his back. Fortunately, he also bent down far enough that she could put her arms around his neck and her legs around his waist. He put a hand around her ankles as his tail curved around her waist, and he rose to a standing position. She immediately realized her mistake. The position pressed her against the broad expanse of his back, his hard muscles rubbing against her still taut nipples. Even worse, she could feel those muscles rippling against her swollen clit.

She started to ease back, about to tell him she had changed her mind, when he leapt into the air. Her arms and legs clenched even tighter around him as they seemed to hang in midair. He landed on a lower branch with an almost imperceptible thud, and then he was off again. The combination of adrenaline and the sheer physical stimulation where their bodies were pressed together overwhelmed her, and to her complete and utter shock, a small climax fluttered through her. She only prayed that Leo hadn't noticed.

CHAPTER SEVEN

Leotra almost missed his hold on the branch he had been aiming at when he heard Lily give a quiet gasp. The scent of her arousal was heavy in the air, and he could feel her slick heat dampening his lower back. He was almost positive that she had just climaxed, but how? No part of him was buried in her body, and she didn't appear to be in heat.

But then again, she had responded deliciously to his mouth earlier and he hadn't caught any hint of artificial heat enhancement then either. Perhaps her species was always ready to mate. The intriguing idea almost made him miss his grip a second time as his cock responded enthusiastically. He did his best to push the idea away and concentrate on the descent.

As soon as his feet were firmly on the ground, he bent down so that she could slide free. He felt her shiver as her damp folds brushed over his ass. When he turned to face her, he could see that her cheeks were flushed and her nipples thrusting against the thin cloth that barely covered her breasts.

He wanted to demand an explanation but remembered his self-imposed limitation just as he opened his mouth. He growled in frustration instead, and her eyes widened—but her scent only increased. Still, there was more than one way to find an answer. He slid a finger between her thighs, almost groaning at the slippery heat that met his touch. Even that one digit seemed too large for her narrow folds as he dragged it through the enticing wetness. A small pearl of flesh at the top of her slit quivered at his touch, and she gasped and took a step back.

"No. No touching."

He lifted the damp finger to his mouth and licked it. Delicious.

"Licking?" he growled.

Those small, blunt teeth closed on her lower lip before she shook her head.

"No licking." Her voice was almost inaudible.

He closed his mouth around his finger, sucking up every last delicious drop.

"Sucking." It wasn't a question. He intended to feast on her.

"N-No."

Despite her denial, her eyes were focused on where he was sucking his finger clean. His tail curved around her waist again. Her hand closed over it, almost automatically, and he bit back another groan. She quickly let it drop, and he wanted to demand that she take hold of him again, but he didn't have the words.

This is ridiculous, he decided. He needed to talk to her. But just as he was about to speak, a low thrumming noise came from the direction of the river. Her eyes lit up.

"That sounds like an engine. Maybe it's a boat."

He was quite sure it was a boat, but there was no reason for one to be present in his territory. Unless it had something to do with her presence.

All of his previous suspicions reappeared. What if she had

been sent here to trap him just like so many other females before her? What if her apparent sexual responsiveness was nothing more than a more sophisticated mating hormone? After all, it wasn't really likely that a female would be constantly receptive. Disappointment, and something that felt strangely like loss, seared through him.

"No," he said gruffly, turning to begin the day's journey.

"What do you mean no?" She ran to catch up with him. "No, it's not a boat? Or an engine?"

Even if he had felt like explaining, he didn't want to use that many words. He simply shook his head and kept walking. It took him longer than it should have before he realized she was no longer following him.

He turned around and found that she was still at the same spot, her hands on her hips as she glared at him. And in spite of everything, that challenging look made his cock throb. She was practically begging for him to pursue her.

"Come," he ordered.

"No. I still think that sounded like an engine, maybe a boat. Which means civilization and, more importantly, the chance of finding my friends." She flicked a hand at him, clearly dismissing him. "So you go your way. I'm going back to the river to find out for sure."

His eyes narrowed and he stomped back towards her, his tail lashing furiously behind him. She didn't run—which was probably just as well under the circumstances since he didn't think he would have been able to overcome his instincts. He would have chased her, and when he caught her, he would have claimed her. *Claimed her?* The mere fact that the thought had occurred to him made him even more furious.

"No boat," he growled, leaning down until their faces were only inches apart.

"Oh, now you know the word boat. I'm beginning to think

you know a hell of a lot more than you're letting on. I'm going to go find that boat."

Oh no she wasn't. He roared, the sound echoing through the jungle, then picked her up and threw her over his shoulder. She gave an outraged cry, swearing at him as she struggled against his grip. Her foot caught him in the stomach, and he promptly smacked her ass. Her whole body went still, and her reaction penetrated his anger. Horrified, he wondered if he had misjudged his strength and hurt her. He gave her ass a soothing stroke, preparing to put her down, and then his thumb brushed across her slit. She was wet, even wetter than she had been before.

With the remnants of his rage still racing through his system, it was all he could do not to carry her to the ground and claim her on the spot. A small rational part of his brain reluctantly reminded him that he still didn't have any answers. The fact that she had responded to one of his favorite sports should only add to his suspicions. And yet he could swear her response was genuine.

Definitely time to get some answers—but first they were getting as far away from the blasted river and any fucking boats as possible. He resumed walking, and she didn't make any further protest. It wasn't until an hour later when they reached the springs and he finally put her down, but he saw her cheeks were stained from crying.

LILY REFUSED TO LOOK AT LEO AS HE GENTLY SET HER back on her feet, disturbed both by her unusual display of emotion and the heat that still lingered in her body. Both of them were strange to her. She'd learned to lock her feelings down a long time ago—even before she'd left home. Her parents were neither affectionate nor even particularly interested in her. No matter what she tried to do to get their attention, their usual response was to ignore her. She had told herself she didn't care and buried the hurt deeper each time. And then when she finally thought she'd found something special with her singer, he'd ended up rejecting her just as easily.

But that was all so long ago. What had released this flood of emotion?

The fact that you're a million miles from home? she thought, but somehow she suspected it was more than that. First she had been taken from a place that she had tentatively started to consider as home, and then from the two women who in a short span of time had become closer to her than anyone ever had. And now she was alone again except for this giant, confusing male. As furious as he made her, somehow she also felt connected to him in a way that made absolutely no sense. Was it just because he had fed her and protected her? Or was it the humor that sparkled in his eyes and the multitude of feelings that flashed across his expressive face?

And why, oh why, was her body responding to him the way it was? She might have been able to explain away her climax when pressed against his back as mere physical stimulation, but the heat that had rushed through her when he smacked her butt had shocked her to her core.

It wasn't that she disliked men—not all of her relationships had been complete disasters—but deep down inside she'd never really trusted them. One or two of her partners had suggested spanking fun, but she had adamantly refused, finding the whole idea appalling. But when this stranger, this alien stranger, had spanked her, she had longed for more.

"Hurt?" Leo asked softly, and she looked up to find him giving her a worried look. *He should be fucking worried*, she thought, but she couldn't muster her usual vehemence. Not when she was still so confused.

"No." She shook her head, then forced herself to add defiantly, "No thanks to you."

She suspected her words rang hollow and didn't like the way he was studying her face, so she deliberately turned away, then gasped in surprise as she noticed their surroundings for the first time.

He had stopped in a secluded clearing. More of the giant trees ringed the space but the area was large enough that sunlight could reach the ground. Soft orange moss covered the ground between a series of rocky pools. Water flowed down a craggy hillside, then from one pool to another before disappearing into the jungle again. Little flowers bloomed amidst the moss while the gentle trickle of water made a soothing backdrop. It was one of the prettiest places she had ever seen.

"This is beautiful," she said softly.

"Beautiful," he echoed, but when she looked up at him, he was looking at her.

The fiery heat that was the curse of the redhead surged to her cheeks, but she ignored it and gave him a suspicious glare instead.

"Your grasp of language certainly seems to be improving. Are you ready to talk?"

He tilted his head, the sunlight glittering in his mane, then nodded. "Talk."

With his startling speed, he picked her up again—cradled against his chest this time—and headed for the largest pool nestled against the small rocky hillside.

"This isn't talking," she muttered, even though she found the way he was carrying her a little too enjoyable. An enjoyment that disappeared when he reached the pool and casually tossed her in. When she rose spluttering to the surface, he was grinning at her triumphantly.

"Why you…" She started towards him, then realized that

the water flowing around her body was warm and silky with a distinct floral scent. The lingering aches in her muscles began to disappear. Distracted from her desire to wreak immediate vengeance, she slowed down and let the water swirl gently around her.

She looked up to find him still standing on the rock at the edge of the pool, the sun highlighting that big golden body and turning him into a mythical creature. Then he tilted his head and grinned at her, white fangs flashing, and he was no longer mythical. He was just her Leo. *Her Leo?* Where the hell had that come from?

But wherever it was, it seemed to have washed her anger away.

"Are you coming in?" she found herself asking.

He dropped his loincloth. She wasn't quite sure exactly what she had expected—some kind of sheath perhaps—but he had the same type of equipment as a human male. Well, not exactly the same. A broad, slightly pointed shaft rose from a thick, textured base. His heavy balls were covered in the same golden fur as the rest of his body. Apparently, pubic hair wasn't part of their anatomy. She wondered what would he think of her own patch of red curls.

She was still staring at his cock in bemusement when he cannonballed into the pool with a huge splash. She spluttered again, then burst out laughing. Ridiculous male.

He surfaced next to her, his damp fur clinging even tighter to those impressive muscles as he grinned down at her.

"I guess you thought I needed a bath?" she said, teasingly.

His expression changed, and he bent down and sniffed her neck.

"No," he growled softly against her skin.

What was it with the sniffing? And why did those little intakes of breath set off little shivers of pleasure?

"I thought you wanted to talk." Her voice came out breathless.

Instead of responding, he picked her up again and walked to one side of the pool. The position of the rocks made a natural bench and he sat there, keeping her firmly on his lap.

"Talk."

It was clearly a command, and she frowned at him. "I thought *you* were going to talk."

He tapped her chest, just above her breasts, and she did her best to ignore the impulse to slide a little higher so he would actually be touching one of the suddenly aching mounds.

"Talk," he repeated.

"All right," she huffed, then hesitated, not exactly sure where to begin. "I'm not from this planet."

He made an odd choking noise, which she realized was a muffled laugh, and she gave him a rueful smile.

"I guess that's obvious. I'm a human and I come from a planet called Earth, but I was taken from there, along with my two friends."

His body had turned rigid beneath her, and she shot a curious glance at his face. He looked angry—no, enraged. A second later, his roar echoed across the clearing, almost deafening her. Why was he so mad?

"It wasn't my fault. I didn't ask to be kidnapped. Are you mad at me?"

"No." Once again, he looked as if he wanted to say something more, but simply shook his head.

"That's really all there is to tell. We'd been on ship for a while, maybe a few weeks, when something happened. I'm not sure what it was, but we were shoved into the escape pods. At least I think we were. They took Kate first, then me, but Mary was still there when they took me away."

Based on the muttered conversation from the slavers, she

was pretty sure that all of them were being sent away from the ship, at least temporarily, but it worried her to think that the other two might still be somewhere on the ship.

He stroked her back in what was obviously intended to be a soothing gesture, but when she looked up at him he was frowning off into the distance. He obviously understood her story, and it just as obviously upset him, but she still wasn't sure why.

She poked her finger at his chest to get his attention. "Now it's your turn. Talk."

He looked down at her, and he was clearly debating with himself, but then he stood up in another one of his swift movements, leaving her alone on the rock bench.

"Food," he said.

"What? That's not fair."

Her words fell on deaf ears. He had already climbed out of the pool. Despite her annoyance, she couldn't help admiring the way the water sparkled on his golden fur before he gave a quick shake and picked up his loincloth.

I never even got another chance to take a closer look at his cock, she thought wistfully before she came to her senses.

He looked back at her, and once again she wondered what he was going to say. But he only shook his head.

"Stay." And then he disappeared out of the clearing.

She glared after him, almost tempted to climb out of the pool and go for a walk just to defy him. But the water really did feel wonderful and it probably wasn't very smart to go wandering around by herself. She took a deep breath and leaned back against the rock instead, letting the water work its magic.

CHAPTER EIGHT

Leotra stomped into the jungle, trying to contain his rage. Someone had stolen her? Taken his fragile female from her home planet and then abandoned her in this wilderness. Wilderness. He came to a sudden halt. The springs should be safe enough—he wasn't aware of any predators that lurked in the waters or frequented the area—but he suddenly felt uneasy about leaving her.

He turned back to the clearing, but after confirming she was still safe in the water, he remained hidden in the undergrowth. There was only one reason she would have been taken —whoever had stolen her had intended to sell her into slavery. For the first time, he recognized that her skimpy outfit had most probably been created from one of the slave gowns typically worn by female slaves. *Slaves.* A snarl rose in his throat.

Slavery was not forbidden under Imperial law, although there were laws governing the treatment of slaves. At one time, his native planet of Yangu had depended on slave labor to mine the gems that had made them so wealthy. But over the years, manual labor had been replaced by machinery and most of

Tajiri society now frowned on the practice. His own grandfather had been one of the first to move away from those methods.

There were even rumors that the new Emperor was considering outlawing slavery, even though it was still a significant economic consideration for many planets. Something tugged his memory. The new Emperor had chosen a consort recently and there were rumors that she was a former slave, from an unknown planet. *Human.* He was sure that had been the term used to describe her—and that was how Lily had identified herself. No wonder she had been taken. There would be many seeking to emulate the Emperor.

Assuming that everything she told you is true, a small cynical voice insisted. He wanted to believe her, he really did, but it wouldn't be the first time that a seemingly helpless female had appeared in his life. He still remembered the delicate little female he'd found crouched on a street corner. She seemed so fragile, half-starved and helpless, and he had whisked her away to his quarters. He lavished her with food and jewels and expensive clothing. He'd been head over heels in love with her, on the verge of claiming her, when he'd heard her laughing with a lover. It had all been part of an elaborate scheme.

Showing up here on his hunting planet seemed farfetched, but was it that much more unlikely? He hadn't seen any signs of this supposed escape pod, although that wasn't a guarantee that it didn't exist. But his guards should have been able to detect the presence of a foreign vessel. And if they had, why hadn't they gone after it?

He sighed, and rubbed his aching head. He wanted to believe her, but the intensity of his feelings already disturbed him. *I need a truth drug,* he thought wryly, leaning back against a moni tree.

A drop of sap dripped on his shoulder, the same sap they had drunk the night before, and a thought suddenly hit him. When left to ripen, the sap developed a mild alcoholic content that, according to his grandfather, caused the drinker to speak the truth. Perhaps a few sips of ripened moni would be enough to make sure she was being honest with him.

This is a bad idea, his conscience told him in a voice uncannily like his grandfather's, but he ignored it. He just needed to know.

Filling another of the cup-shaped leaves with the sap, he placed it on a rock at the edge of the clearing in full sun to hasten the ripening process. But he had also promised to return with food. There wasn't as much game as he would have liked within earshot of the clearing, but he managed to capture one of the long, sinuous reptiles that liked to hide amongst the vines and snag unwary prey.

When he returned triumphant to the clearing, Lily was still in the healing pool. Her head was tilted up to the sun, sunlight creating sparks of fire in her glorious hair, and those small yet full lips curved in a provocative smile. He stood at the edge of the pool looking down at her, her thin outfit so translucent in the clear water that he could see the pink areola surrounding her luscious little nipples and the tempting little patch of fur between her legs. Was she posed like that on purpose, knowing what an enticing picture she made?

In spite of his doubts, his cock responded, throbbing hard enough against his loincloth that it threatened to escape. He grunted and tried to push it back under the leather covering, and Lily's eyes popped open. The provocative smile disappeared as she glared at him.

"You told me we were going to talk. That meant you too."

Gods help him, her anger turned him on even more, and he gave up the useless battle to contain his cock. As soon as his hand dropped, her eyes focused there and that provocative little tongue flicked across her lips. If he had been anyone else, if he had any other experiences, he would have sworn the desire on her face was genuine. He took a half-step closer, then forced himself to maintain the discipline his grandfather had taught him, discipline that still lurked beneath his privileged façade.

"Food," he said, pointing his claw at the reptile.

A Tajiri female would have known that it was a difficult predator to catch and would have admired his skills. Lily recoiled.

"A snake? That's your idea of food?" She shuddered and shook her head. "I don't think I can eat that raw, no matter how thinly you slice it."

It seemed a waste, but if she preferred her food cooked, he would oblige. He returned to the edge of the clearing, gathering dry branches and loose undergrowth. By the time he had a pile assembled on a flat rock, Lily had abandoned the pool and come to join him. Her outfit was only slightly less translucent out of the water, and he wanted to lick his lips at the sight of her. She caught him looking and glared, her hands going to her hips.

"If you don't like it, you shouldn't have thrown me into the water. It's not as if I have another outfit to wear."

An immediate—and foolish—desire to promise her a thousand outfits almost made it out of his mouth, but he caught it in time. He still had a role to play.

He took a step closer, noting approvingly that she didn't flinch away from him, and dipped his head into the bend of her neck where he could breathe in her enticing scent.

"Like," he growled.

He felt her shiver, and when he stepped back, those impudent nipples formed hard little points against the damp cloth. He wanted to taste them again—Gods, how he wanted to taste them—but he needed to know the truth first. He returned to his collection of wood.

L<small>ILY GLARED AT</small> L<small>EO AS HE TURNED AWAY FROM HER AND</small> bent down over his fire. How could he do that to her—set every nerve in her body on fire just by sniffing her neck? Her foot itched, urging her to push him over from his crouched position, but in the end she reconsidered. Based on what she had seen before, she doubted she would succeed and she suspected he would retaliate.

Another wave of desire washed through her at the thought of wrestling with him. She knew it would end up with her pinned beneath him and her clit actually gave an excited little pulse at the thought. *What is wrong with me?*

She shook her head and started to take a step back, but before she could, something warm curved around her calf. For a horrified moment, she thought it was another snake, but when she looked down she realized it was his tail, squeezing her leg in what almost seemed to be an apology. Curious, she crouched down behind him and took his tail in her hand as she had the previous day. The fur here was even softer than that on his body, warm over the thick length of muscle and she stroked it, squeezing gently. He whirled around so quickly that he almost fell.

His mouth fell open in combination of shock and outrage, but she saw the head of his cock pushing up past the waistband of his loincloth again. Hmm, so it was an erogenous zone.

"Tail," she said innocently. "Just another language lesson."

He tried to snatch it away from her, but she held on tight enough that he was forced to tug it out of her grip, the muscle flexing beneath her hand until she came to the ridiculously soft and fluffy tip.

"No," he growled, but she didn't think he sounded any more convincing than she had when she told him not to suck on her nipples that morning.

Feeling unexpectedly triumphant, she shrugged and moved back a little. It was nice to know that she had her own weapons in whatever game he was playing. She just wished she knew the purpose of his game. She was almost positive that he understood everything she said, and even though he still insisted on his limited one-word vocabulary, she was beginning to suspect that he could choose to make himself understood.

All of which made her want to glare at him again—but then again, he was making a fire he obviously didn't need just for her. He was still doing his best to protect her. Even throwing her into the pool could be interpreted as a desire to make her feel better. The water had soothed away the lingering aches and bruises from the crash.

She stretched out on the soft moss to let her outfit dry in the warm sun, and tried to come up with a plan. Unfortunately, she had never been much of a planner—she tended to drift whichever way the wind took her.

Kate would have a plan, she thought idly, then her throat closed. She needed to find her friends. That meant she needed to get tall, golden, and gorgeous to communicate with her. *Maybe I should seduce him.* The wicked little suggestion flickered through her mind. It wouldn't exactly be a hardship, she decided, turning over on her side to watch his muscles flex.

"How are you going to start that fire?" she asked challengingly. She had no doubt that he had a plan, but she liked the way he looked offended whenever she challenged him.

He looked over at her and raised that eyebrow again before holding up a small black stone. Holding it close to the pile of dried brush, he let one of his claws emerge, then struck it against the stone a few times. A spark landed in the brush, smoldered, then started to burn.

Oh my. When he turned and grinned at her triumphantly, she couldn't prevent herself from smiling back.

"I should have known."

"Yes," he agreed as he picked up the snake.

He used the same claw to slit open the skin, but she really didn't want to watch this part. She rolled over on her back again and watched the leaves swaying against the pink sky.

CHAPTER NINE

The smell of roasting meat penetrated Lily's senses, and she realized she must have fallen asleep again. Even locked in a cage, she had been too nervous to sleep on the ship, but she apparently felt safe in the middle of a jungle with a huge alien lion man. Why did she feel so certain that he would never let anything happen to her?

Shaking her head at her own foolishness, she stretched lazily, then looked over at the fire. Strips of snake meat had been wound around thin branches and then arranged over the fire. The smell made her mouth water and now that it was simply pieces of meat, it was easier to forget where it had come from.

"That smells wonderful," she murmured, and Leo looked up from where he was crouched by the fire.

He smiled at her, blue eyes sparkling, and her stomach did an odd little flip. *Fuck.* Why did he have to be so attractive? It didn't seem to matter anymore that he was an alien.

But what does matter is that he's keeping secrets from me, she reminded herself.

Remembering her earlier plan, she stood and stretched languidly, making sure he had a clear view. He watched her hungrily—perhaps a little too hungrily because her body immediately responded to the look in his eyes. Seducing answers out of him without getting seduced herself might be a little bit tricky.

Determined to remain in control, she sauntered over to the fire, letting her hips swing provocatively. She put her hand on his shoulder and bent down to take an appreciative whiff, knowing that the position made her breasts almost overflow her makeshift top.

"How long until it's ready?" she asked, her voice low and husky.

"Ready," he growled, his gaze fixed on her cleavage. His tail curved around her calf again.

"Then we should eat."

"Yes." He looked up at her face, then deliberately swiped his tongue across his lips, and she knew he wasn't thinking about food. Her traitorous nipples hardened immediately, but she refused to acknowledge them. She buried her hand in his mane and tugged gently.

"Then what are you waiting for?"

A low grumble emerged from his throat and for a moment, she wondered if she had pushed him too far. But then he shook his head and reached for one of the skewers of meat. He started to hand it to her, then paused and picked up what looked like a crumbled leaf and scattered it over the skewer first.

She took it with a suspicious frown but he only cocked an eyebrow, daring her to taste it. She took a cautious bite, then groaned with pleasure. It tasted almost exactly like grilled chicken, and she realized the crumbled leaf added a slight salty note.

"Salt," he said smugly.

An unexpected lump appeared in her throat. He had not only paid attention to her comment from the previous night, but he had made the effort to please her. But then her pleasure was replaced by suspicion. He had understood that, just as he seemed to understand everything else. So why wouldn't he talk to her?

"What kind of plant is that?" she asked casually.

"Chuv."

"Where does it grow? Is it hard to find?"

Peeping at him from under her lashes, she saw his mouth open, then close again. Did he look amused?

"No."

He was back to his one-word answers, and she sighed. She looked over at him in time to see him wipe a smile from his face. Hmm. They would just have to see about that.

Once her stomach was full, he arranged the remaining skewers higher over the fire and added some damp leaves to the coals to make them smoke. Her minimal scouting experience came to the rescue.

"Are you curing the meat?"

He shot her a quick glance, then nodded.

"How did you learn how to do this?"

When he didn't answer immediately she casually picked up his tail and stroked her fingers down the thick length.

"Grandfather," he said, his voice strangled, and gave her a reproachful look.

"Are we going any further today?" She remembered he had said it was two days to reach his home, but she wasn't exactly surprised when he shook his head. Did he even have a home?

Aside from the worry about her friends, she didn't really object to spending the rest of the day in this pleasant little clearing. Maybe she could use the time to finally get some answers.

"Maybe we should use the time to work on your language skills," she said innocently as she squeezed his tail.

Once again, he pulled it free, but she kept her hand closed so that it slid down the entire length. Was his cock covered in fur? She tried to remember that brief glance. It had been the same color as his fur but it had gleamed in the sunlight.

He was giving her suspicious looks, so she leaned closer and found the small pointed ear half-hidden in his wild mane.

"Ear," she whispered, closing her teeth delicately over the velvety soft skin. He shuddered.

This is going to be fun, she thought, but then he tugged her into his lap and his rough tongue licked the delicate shell of her ear, sending a streak of lightning down her spine.

"Ear." The low purr of his voice made her shiver, but she refused to give in. Then his mouth moved down to her neck, and he gave an inquiring grunt.

"Neck," she gasped.

"Neck," he purred. He licked her there as well, sending little flickers of excitement rocketing through her body. This game was rapidly getting out of hand.

She pushed against his chest, and he immediately released her. When she stood, her pussy was directly in front of his face. His hands went to her hips, keeping her there as he leaned closer. He nudged the scrap of white fabric aside, revealing her red curls. Her hands went to those big golden shoulders, but she didn't push him away.

"What do you call that?" She tried to sound confident, but her voice shook.

"Cunt," he growled. "Delicious cunt."

She should have felt triumphant that she'd managed to get

two consecutive words out of him, but she was too focused on that big head so close to where she needed him. He took a deep breath, an almost ecstatic expression on his face, then released it, the rush of warm air making her shudder as it reached her damp curls.

"Wet." His finger traced a path through her curls, barely touching her, but she was so sensitized that she almost came from that single touch. "Always wet."

His hands suddenly clenched on her hips, and she felt the faintest prick of his claws before he released her so quickly she almost stumbled.

"Food," he said abruptly, turning towards the jungle. He took a step in that direction, then looked back at her over his shoulder. She was quite sure she was giving him an open-mouth stare.

He sighed and reached for his belt, and she wondered if he was going to take her, right here and right now. And why didn't that thought terrify her?

To her relief—and disappointment—all he did was hand her the strap with his knife attached.

"Why? Are you leaving me?" The question tumbled out before she could prevent it. Dammit. She wasn't going to beg him to stay.

He shook his head. "Protection."

Her hand trembled as she took it. "Why do I need protection? Isn't this place safe?"

"Yes." He didn't sound quite as reassuring as she would have liked, especially when he pointed to the snakeskin drying in the sun. "But..."

Great. Her hand tightened on the hilt of the knife. The idyllic spot no longer looked quite so idyllic.

"But you're coming back, right?"

"Yes." With one of his lightning-fast moves, he hauled her up against his body and brushed his lips against hers. "More language."

And then he disappeared into the jungle, leaving her confused, annoyed, and extremely horny.

CHAPTER TEN

Once again, Leotra retreated into the jungle. He wasn't angry this time, only confused. He still had no idea what to make of Lily. The fact that she had been touching him so seductively argued that she was trying to manipulate him, but it did seem to be in an effort to get him to talk. And he—and his ever-ready cock—had enjoyed the game.

But then he had been so close to her delicious little cunt, close enough to see the sparkle of her essence in those red curls. She was so clearly sexually receptive, wet and ready for him. He couldn't detect even a hint of mating hormone beneath her intoxicating fragrance, but how was it possible? Was he just lucky enough to have encountered her during her heat? And if that was so, how long would it last? Or was it all some deliciously baited trap?

His every instinct urged him to trust her, but his instincts had been wrong before.

Tonight. Tonight, they would share the moni sap and he would find out the truth. In the meantime, he would hunt for her. Although there was enough smoked meat to provide a second meal, his female deserved a fresh kill. *Fuck.* No, not his female. At least not yet...

When he returned to the clearing, she hadn't moved from where he left her. Her hand was clenched around the knife, and her eyes were scanning the trees. Fuck, he hadn't intended to scare her. He had thought that having the knife would reassure her.

But even though he hated the idea that she had been scared, he loved the way her eyes lit up when she saw him.

"There you are. And—oh my God, is that a bunny rabbit?"

The word didn't translate and he lifted his kill by its long ears. "Sungura."

She waved her hand, her face pale. "If you say so. It looks like a bunny to me. I really don't think I'm cut out for primitive living."

Perhaps it was time to bring this expedition to a close. His imagination immediately conjured up a picture of her sprawled naked against his sheets while he fed her the choicest tidbits at his disposal. His finger hovered over the communicator concealed in his loincloth, but then he pulled it away. What if this was just the beginning? Would a demand for clothing and jewelry follow?

He had never seen an avaricious look in her eyes, and her muttered comment had been barely audible, but once again his suspicions were triggered. The sooner he knew the truth, the better. With that in mind, he began cleaning his kill.

Lily studiously averted her eyes as he did, but when he wrapped pieces of the meat in more leaves and buried them in the hot coals, she came to join him, studying the cooking process with interest.

"Did your grandfather teach you that as well?"

He nodded wistfully. He had spent so much time here with his grandfather while the older man taught him the ways of the jungle. It had always been just the two of them—his grandfather would have laughed himself breathless at the size of the retinue that usually accompanied his father. And now him. When had that changed? About the time he reached maturity and his father began inserting himself into Leotra's life.

Lily patted his tail, and this time her touch was sympathetic rather than seductive.

"I'm sorry. You must miss him very much."

He nodded, then frowned. How would she know that they had been out of touch for the last few years? Time to start asking questions of his own.

"You?"

"You mean do I have a grandfather? I suppose I must have, but I never met him." A mixture of sadness and anger crossed her face. "I bet my parents weren't any more interested in their parents than they were in me."

"Not interested?" He almost groaned at his response, but she was gazing out into the jungle again, her expression distant.

"Let's just say I'm not sure why they ever bothered to have a child. Either it was an accident, or they thought that it was a requirement."

Her words created an unwilling spark of sympathy. He barely remembered his mother, just a fleeting smile and a trace of perfume, but he was quite sure that his father had only sired a child because it was expected of him. He hadn't shown any interest in Leotra either, but at least he'd had his grandfather. It didn't seem as if Lily had had anyone.

"Sorry," he said softly, patting her hand the same way she had patted his tail.

She shrugged, clearly dismissing the memories. "It's not your fault. Some people should just never have children. I'm probably one of them."

Despite her denial, he could easily envision her lush and

glowing with his cub inside her. His cock reacted enthusiastically to the image, a sudden deep, instinctual urge to mate her and fill her with his seed sweeping over him. Thank the gods he'd had his fertility restricted since his fourteenth birthday. Since it would be the easiest way to trap him, he had never trusted a female to prevent a pregnancy.

"More," he urged her.

"More what?"

"More you. Life."

Her puzzled frown disappeared in a triumphant laugh. "Ha. That's three words in a row. I'm winning you over."

She most certainly is, he thought.

While the sunjura meat cooked, he started working on the skin. Another one of his grandfather's lessons—no part of a kill should be wasted. Another tenet to which his father paid little heed. He had no hesitation in killing an animal for just one specific organ.

Why was he thinking so much about his grandfather? Perhaps because this had always been their special time together. He frowned as he realized just how long it had been since he'd seen the older male.

"Is everything all right?" Lily's soft fingers brushed across his arm.

"Thinking," he said with a shrug.

"I don't suppose you want to share those thoughts?"

He actually would have liked to get her perspective, but not yet.

"More life," he said instead, poking her gently on her chest and fighting back the urge to linger on her soft skin.

She had been telling him about a singer who had enticed her away from her home at what seemed to be a disturbingly young age.

"So then he decided he didn't want a relationship

anymore," she continued, smiling ruefully. "I was such a child. I thought my heart was going to break."

He had taken her from her home and then rejected the mating? The unworthy male's behavior appalled him—and yet she was free as a result. Or was she? She certainly hadn't mentioned anyone else, and he found himself curiously reluctant to ask. Perhaps it was time to try the ripened sap.

He finished scraping the fur and stretched it out to dry in the late afternoon sunlight, then collected the leaf holding the moni sap. The liquid had thickened and ripened just as he planned. As he brought it back over to her, he was seized by an unexpected reluctance. He wanted to believe she was exactly who she seemed to be. He didn't want to test her, and if she was lying, he wasn't sure he wanted to know the truth.

She looked up at him expectantly, her beautiful face open and trusting, but the very strength of his desire to believe her made him suspicious. Perhaps she was drugging him after all. Was her scent so seductive because she was using some new mating hormone?

He sat next to her on the rock, offering her the leaf, and their hands brushed as she took it from him. Even that fleeting touch sent an ache of desire straight to his cock. Surely, this could not be a natural reaction.

"Mmm, is this what we had before? It tastes different somehow."

She licked her lips, and he was mesmerized by the sight of that small pink tongue. It took him much longer than it should have before he realized that she had asked him a question.

"Ripened." His voice sounded hoarse.

She handed the leaf back to him, and he took a thirsty gulp as she studied him. Then she tapped thoughtfully at her chin with her small, blunt nail.

"You know, ripened isn't exactly a basic word. You can speak better than you have been, can't you?"

"Yes." *Fuck.* He hadn't considered the fact that the truth effect would work on him as well.

"I see. Then why aren't you talking to me?"

"Trap." The word escaped before he could prevent it, but he slammed his mouth close.

A tiny furrow appeared on her brow, and he longed to smooth it away. Instead, he tried to change the subject.

"After singer?"

"And now you're changing the subject. You have a lot of secrets, don't you, Leo?"

Unwilling to trust his voice, he simply shrugged, and she frowned again.

"I'm not sure why you're so interested in my ordinary life."

"Interested in you."

Perhaps she read the truth on his face, because her expression softened.

"You really can be very sweet."

He fought back a feeling of guilt as she continued with her story. He really did not like that sensation, but it only intensified as she spoke. Although she tried to make light of it, from what he could tell her life had been a long series of betrayals. She had never found a home or a worthy male to protect her. The only time she revealed any genuine affection was when she spoke of the two females who had also been taken by the slavers.

By the time she finished her story, night had fallen. They had finished their dinner, along with the last of the moni sap, and he had no doubt at all that she was exactly who she claimed to be. Which meant that he no longer needed to resist the temptation she presented.

He would take care of her, he vowed. He would provide

her with suitable clothing and jewelry and introduce her into his social circle. But first, he would attempt to find her friends. It should present little problem for a male with his resources, and he could already anticipate her gratitude.

He opened his mouth to tell her of his plans for her, and she crawled into his lap. His thoughts shattered as all the blood in his body went to his cock. Her delicate skin was softer than his finest silk robes and infinitely more enticing. She nestled into his arms, and his head spun with her provocative scent and the last remnants of the sap.

CHAPTER ELEVEN

Somehow, Lily had ended up in Leo's arms, but she didn't mind. A warm glow of contentment suffused her body. She felt so close to him. Even though he had still revealed little about himself he had listened sympathetically to her life story. He even seemed angry on her behalf at the way the men in her life had treated her.

"Beautiful Lily," he murmured against her ear, and then his mouth went to her neck. God, she loved that. But despite the excitement shivering through her body, she wanted to explore him.

She swung around in his lap, running her fingers through the sleek fur covering his broad chest. She found his small copper-colored nipples and twisted them playfully. He growled, but it didn't sound like a protest. Her fingers dipped lower, finding the head of his cock pushing up to meet her from beneath the waistband of his loincloth.

As golden as his fur, she thought dreamily, but when she swiped her thumb across the top, it was smooth and hot. A little pearl of fluid appeared, and she gathered it up with her finger, popping it into her mouth. She closed her eyes and sighed happily. Delicious. Like salted caramel. She thought she heard him groan, but she was determined to see more. She fumbled with the loincloth, trying to free his erection, but his big hand covered hers.

"Are you sure?"

Something about his voice sounded different, but she was too impatient to care. She tugged on the scrap of leather again, and he groaned. Then he unfastened some hidden knot and the leather fell away. His cock sprang free, huge and thick and perfect. She ran a curious finger over the small protrusions that covered the wide base and he groaned. They had an almost rubbery texture that teased her fingertips. The thought of feeling them inside her sent arousal rushing through her body, even though she wasn't sure that her channel could stretch far enough to take the swollen base.

"What are these?" she whispered.

"My barbs."

That sounded painful, but when she ran her finger across them again, they moved against her in a way that promised pleasure rather than pain.

"What are they for?"

"To hold my female in place as I plant my seed."

Part of her mind thought that it sounded barbaric, but it didn't prevent a wave of excitement flooding her empty pussy. Then she frowned.

"That was a whole sentence."

"Yes," he growled in her ear as his mouth dropped to her neck again. He lapped at the precise spot that made her quiver, his rough tongue adding to the sensation, and her question suddenly seemed less important than exploring the physical connection between them.

She wound her fingers in the thick silk of his mane and tugged gently until he raised his head.

"Kiss me," she demanded.

His eyes blazed blue fire as his mouth came down over hers. Oh my God. This was nothing like the brush against her lips that he had given her before. Either his people were seriously good kissers, or he was an unnaturally quick study. He thrust his tongue into her mouth the same way she imagined he would thrust that enormous cock into her pussy. He growled against her mouth, tangling his fingers in her hair to hold her in place as he delved deeper.

One of his fangs caught her lip, and he immediately licked away the light sting, groaning with pleasure. A big hand closed over her breast, kneading the soft mound as his thumb stroked across her nipple. The thick length of his tail curled around her thigh, tugging it open as his other hand cupped her mound. A searing wave of heat raced through her.

"So wet," he growled. "Are you in heat?"

Dazed by pleasure, she struggled to make sense of the question.

"I don't think so."

"Human females are always this receptive?"

Something about the question bothered her, but then he brushed his thumb across her clit and her thoughts went up like sparks of fire.

"Only for the right man," she managed to stutter as he slid a thick digit into her empty channel.

"And I am the right male."

The smug satisfaction in his voice penetrated, and she started to frown up at him.

"Just as you are the right female," he added. "My female."

The dark, possessive growl made her channel tighten around his finger, and he groaned approvingly.

"That's right. Squeeze me with that sweet little cunt."

He made one of his lightning-fast moves, and then she was on her back in the soft moss. He leaned over her, firelight turning the edges of his mane to liquid gold. His thumb continued to circle her clit as his finger thrust into her with a steady, demanding rhythm.

"Come for me, love," he ordered. "Let me feel you milking my fingers."

His mouth closed over a throbbing nipple as he added a second thick finger, and she arched helplessly against him as a shockingly intense climax swept over her body. She had always considered sex pleasurable, but this wasn't anything as mild as pleasure—this was a far more overwhelming sensation. She was still seeing sparks behind her eyes when she felt the thick head of his cock at her entrance. She expected him to plunge into her but when he didn't, she opened her eyes and saw him looking down at her. The flickering light from the dying fire made it difficult to read his face, but she could feel the intensity in his gaze.

"Do you accept me?"

Her head was still spinning, but she didn't have any doubts. She wanted him inside her.

"Yes," she whispered.

His cock surged forward, but even as wet and ready as she was, her body resisted the massive intrusion. He groaned.

"Your cunt is perfect. Perfectly hot, perfectly tight."

She could feel her body beginning to stretch around him as he tried to work his way deeper.

"Almost too tight," he panted. "Open for me, love."

Once again, her body reacted to that demanding growl, and she instinctively tried to raise her hips.

"Yes, just like that. I'm going to fill you so full." He reached between their bodies and pressed his thumb against her clit.

She could hear the satisfaction in his voice as her channel fluttered in response. He pushed deeper, keeping his promise, filling her.

"Halfway there," he groaned, and her eyes flew open.

Only half? But then he pressed forward again, and she realized she had forgotten that thick textured base. The small protrusions raked across her inside walls, and she saw stars again. *Too big,* a distant part of her mind protested, but the stinging stretch of his intrusion only added to the heat racing through her system. Another climax swept over her, her channel convulsing around his massive shaft.

She heard him roar as the increased wetness eased his way and he finally filled her completely. Sensations overwhelmed her—the enormous throbbing heat of his cock, the soft moss caressing her back, even the warm air stroking her exposed skin. Her climax never seemed to end, pulse after pulse of heat roaring through her, echoing the pulse of his cock as it throbbed inside her. She felt it expand, felt it gripping her, but the pleasure was too much. The stars spun overhead, and she felt huge fur-covered arms close around her, holding her against him as she started to slip into darkness.

She could have sworn she heard him whispering to her, telling her that she was beautiful and perfect and his. She knew it was only a dream, but it made her happy.

"I'm yours," she whispered back as she fell asleep.

CHAPTER TWELVE

Leo's face was in Lily's neck again when she awoke. The clearing was filled with dappled light, and she realized that she had slept all night long. Something about the previous night demanded her attention, but it slipped away as he licked her neck with that wonderfully rough tongue. She shivered, and he lifted up over her and smiled down at her. His fangs flashed white, but she didn't care, especially when she remembered how good they felt scraping across her swollen nipples.

"Good morning, love," he whispered, and then he kissed her.

Fuck. It was every bit as erotic and sensual as she remembered, his rough tongue twining with hers as he explored her mouth. A low, persistent ache started between her thighs, and she tried to arch up against him. He chuckled, the deep sound making his chest reverberate against the tight points of her nipples. He abandoned her mouth, kissing his way down her body. Her breasts quivered in anticipation, but aside from one slow, thorough pull at each needy peak, he kept moving. He obviously had a different destination in mind.

Her breath caught as he pushed her thighs apart, his big hands easily spanning her flesh and the faint prickle of his claws a teasing reminder. He paused for a moment, studying her pussy. She would have been embarrassed if she hadn't been so eager for him to continue.

"Beautiful," he breathed and the hot rush of his breath against the damp flesh made her cry out. "That's my girl."

Something stirred in her memory, but then he swept that wonderful tongue from her weeping pussy to her throbbing clit and everything else disappeared. He feasted on her as hungrily as he had feasted on her mouth, his tongue everywhere, circling the throbbing little pearl of flesh and dipping far too quickly into her empty channel. By the time he focused on her clit and thrust a thick finger deep inside her, all she could do was clench her hands in his mane and hold on as her body exploded.

"Yes," he growled. "Always so hot and wet and ready for me."

His cock was notched at the entrance to her pussy before her brain finally began to work.

"Wait a minute, wait a minute!" she cried.

His cockhead pushed inside, stretching her in that wonderfully exciting way she remembered from the previous night, but he paused and looked up at her.

"Yes, love? Are you sore from yesterday?"

"No. Well, maybe a little but that's not the point. When did you suddenly start speaking in complete sentences?"

He flashed her his cocky grin and slid another inch inside her. She fought back the urge to moan.

"Don't worry, I'll take it easy on you. Slow and steady," he added as if reminding himself.

Her hips wanted to roll up to meet him, but she forced herself to hold still.

"That's not what I'm worried about. Why are you talking to me now?"

"I explained that last night," he said absently. His eyes were focused on where their bodies joined as he pressed deeper. "Your sweet little cunt is so small, but look at the way it stretches to take me."

Fuck. The dirty words in his deep, growling voice combined with the increasing stretch had her seeing stars, but she did her best to concentrate.

"No. I don't remember."

His hips snapped forward another inch and they both groaned, but her words finally seemed to penetrate and he looked back up at her, frowning.

"You really don't remember?"

She did her best to ignore the desire thrumming through her body and tried to recall. Why was it so hazy? She suddenly remembered the cup of sap he kept passing her.

"What was in that drink?" she demanded.

An almost imperceptible expression of guilt flashed across his face, and her heart sank.

"It was ripened moni sap, just like I told you. I explained it to you last night."

The memory hovered just out of reach. There was something, something about being trapped.

"You thought I was trying to trick you," she said slowly.

"That's right." He smiled again, but it wasn't the cocky grin this time. Instead, it was warm and soft and made her chest ache. "But you were exactly who you said you were."

"But you weren't," she whispered.

His gaze snapped back to hers.

"What do you mean?"

"You tricked me. You pretended to be someone else." More

of her memories were returning, and an increasing anger mingled with her despair. "You made me waste three days when I could have been searching for my friends because you're a rich, spoiled prick."

He drew back as if she had slapped him. His cock slipped free, and even now, a foolish demanding part of her body regretted the loss.

"I knew I wanted to claim you the moment I saw you," he protested. "I just had to be sure."

"And it never occurred to you that I might want to be sure as well? Do you know how many men have lied to me? I actually thought you were different."

"Lily, love, let me explain. I never intended to hurt you."

He looked so sincerely upset that she almost reconsidered, but her battered heart just couldn't take anymore.

"And to top it all off, you tried to get me drunk."

The expression of horror on his face was almost convincing.

"I would never do such a thing. The moni sap only reveals the truth. It would never cause you to say or do something you didn't genuinely want to do."

"You claimed me." That memory was crystal clear. "You said I was yours. And you were drinking it too."

"As I said, it only makes you speak the truth."

She wanted to believe him, but too many emotions were warring within her.

"I have to—"

The sound of an engine interrupted her. Leo looked up, then quickly gathered up her discarded clothing and passed it to her.

"Get dressed. We're about to have company."

"Company?"

"Yes. I sent a message last night asking for us to be picked up today. Once I realized you were telling the truth—" he winced guiltily "—I knew that we needed to arrange a search for your friends. And we can't do that from here."

She was still staring at him in shock and he growled impatiently, pulling her to her feet and trying to fasten her outfit back in place.

"As much as I hate to cover up this delightful body, no one sees what is mine."

"I never said I was yours."

He had started to turn away to pick up his loincloth, but he turned back at her quiet words and pulled her against him, lifting her chin so that she was looking directly into his face.

"Yes, you did, Lily. And it was the truth."

LEOTRA FUMED SILENTLY AS THE HOVERCOPTER CARRIED them back to his lodge. He didn't like the speculative way his two Bukharan guards were eyeing Lily. He tugged her closer against his side, trying to angle his position so that less of her delicious body was visible. She was still stiff in his arms, but fortunately she didn't resist.

He was afraid that if she did, the primitive instincts that she aroused would have urged him to claim her again, no matter who was present. But more than that, he missed the soft willing Lily from last night—and this morning before she started to question him. Had she truly not remembered? Was it possible that the moni sap acted differently on humans? What if she hadn't spoken the truth?

No. He refused to believe that. She had told him that she belonged to him and he refused to accept any other possibility.

When they reached his lodge, she barely reacted. He had

been sure she would be impressed by the luxurious surroundings, but she barely gave them a glance, walking stiffly next to him as he hurried her to his quarters. He would even have preferred fiery, challenging Lily to this stiff little automaton.

"Master Leotra?" Hudomo asked, hurrying along behind him. "Is everything all right? I would have sent a hovercopter for you earlier, but your message said that you wished to be alone." He shot a curious glance at Lily, then coughed discreetly. "Would you like me to arrange transport for your... companion?"

The implication horrified him, and rage washed over Leotra's vision as he turned, looming over Hudomo as his claws flexed.

"You will use respect when you speak of Mistress Lily."

"Mi... Mistress Lily?"

Fuck. He hadn't intended to announce that quite so quickly, especially with Lily acting the way she was. It would be all over the household within an hour and undoubtedly spreading to Yangu before the end of the day.

But it was too late now, and he refused to have any regrets. She was his.

"Yes," he bit. "Now send an assortment of food and drink to my sitting room. Make sure all the meat is cooked. And send a female servant as well. Have her wait in the sitting area until I send for her."

Hudomo nodded nervously and hurried off, and Leotra turned to find Lily glaring at him. Oh yes, that was much better.

"Is something wrong?"

"I can't believe you just told him to send somebody to stand around and wait for you."

"Actually, she will be waiting for you."

"For me?"

"Yes." He took a step closer and bent his head, breathing in her soothing scent. "As much as I enjoy the outfit you are wearing, I assume you would prefer more clothing."

Her breath stuttered, and he smiled. No matter what she said with her words, her body already recognized him as her mate.

She pushed at him with her tiny fist, and he obligingly stepped back.

"What about my friends?"

"I will check to see if there's any information as soon as we reach my—*our*—rooms."

For the first time, she seemed to actually notice her surroundings. Her eyes traveled over the inlaid wood floor to the tasteful sculptures set in niches along the corridor. Unfortunately, she still didn't look either pleased or impressed. If anything, she looked more annoyed.

"I wasn't wrong when I called you a rich, spoiled... person, was I?" she muttered.

"Actually, you called me a rich, spoiled prick." He stepped closer again, crowding her against the front of his body. "If I understand the translation protocol correctly, you were actually referring to my cock. Which is not rich, but was undoubtedly spoiled by your hot little cunt. I can't wait to spoil him again with another delicious taste of you."

Her eyes widened, and he could feel the hard little tips of her breasts branding his chest before he stepped back.

"Whenever you're ready, of course," he added.

She gave the most delightful little growl, and he laughed, suddenly sure that this was going to work out after all.

"Now, we're going to go to our rooms and I'm going to bathe you and feed you and dress you while we see if we can find out what happened to your friends."

Still glaring up at him, she didn't move. He pretended to

sigh as he gently turned her in the right direction, then smacked her ass. She jumped, and the smell of her arousal flooded the corridor as she started walking.

Oh, yes, this was going to be perfect.

CHAPTER THIRTEEN

Two hours later, Leotra was cursing the gods, his ancestors, and his own temerity in assuming that it would be a simple matter to win Lily back into his arms. Nothing had gone the way he'd planned.

She hadn't been any more impressed by the luxury of his quarters than she had been by the rest of the lodge. He had envisioned bathing her in the enormous pool attached to his room. Instead, she had ordered him to leave while she bathed herself.

"This is my bathing room," he reminded her.

"Fine. Then I'll leave you to use it."

"Don't you want to get clean?"

"Yes. By myself."

They had glared at each other until he threw up his hands and stomped away. Stubborn female.

Then when she emerged after her bath, she was wrapped in a towel rather than one of the outfits he had chosen for her from the selection Hudomo had provided.

"Why didn't you put on one of the gowns?"

"Why should I?" She sniffed disdainfully. "I don't want to wear one of your other lover's castoffs."

"They don't belong to another lover," he roared.

"Then where did they come from?"

He scowled, but finally admitted, "I don't know. Hudomo arranged for them. But I have never seen any of them on another female."

She didn't seem convinced. In the end, he settled the matter by letting her choose something from his own wardrobe. Although having her dressed in one of his shirts was surprisingly... satisfactory, he wanted to see her in clothing that suited her beauty.

He was still irritated when they entered his sitting area—and the situation got even worse. A maidservant knelt by the selection of foods on a low table, but at their entrance she rose gracefully to her feet and slinked towards them. She completely ignored Lily as she came over to him, stopping a little too close.

"I'm ready to serve you, Master Leotra," she purred.

Her behavior wasn't completely unexpected—most of the female servants had tried to seduce him at one point or another. Usually he just ignored them, then had Hudomo remove them from any duties that involved direct contact with him.

"You are here to attend to Mistress Lily," he said, his voice cold.

The wretched female didn't even look at his mate.

"Of course, Master Leotra. But I am prepared to attend to your needs as well."

To his astonishment, he heard Lily make an odd little growling noise as she stepped in front of him.

"He doesn't need you to serve him, and I certainly don't. Leave."

The female looked shocked, but then her fangs flashed and

he saw her claws emerge. He immediately tugged Lily back behind him.

"If you dare to lay a single claw on my female, there is no place where you will escape my wrath. Your mistress told you to leave. Now do so."

He was roaring by the time he finished.

She hissed and shrank back, ducking her head.

"I—I apologize, Master. I was misinformed."

He was too enraged to have any patience with her attempt to apologize.

"Leave." he ordered, and she fled the room.

"I'm sorry, love," he said, turning back to Lily.

He expected her to be angry, or even frightened, but instead she looked oddly thoughtful.

"Are they all like that?"

"Like what?"

"Fawning all over you."

"Of course not—" He stopped, then sighed. "Not all, but many of them. My father expects all servants to be accommodating."

"You mean he expects them to have sex with him?" she asked bluntly.

He started to deny it, but hesitated again. "He wouldn't demand it—" at least he hoped not "—but most female servants in a household like ours would regard it as an honor."

Or a way to earn rewards, he thought cynically.

Lily snorted. "Yeah, right. It's such an honor to suck your dick, Master Leo."

Even though she was obviously being sardonic, his cock flexed at the image of her taking him in her little pink mouth. His thoughts must have shown on his face, because she took a step back, holding up her hands.

"That wasn't an offer."

He followed her retreat, curving his tail around her waist so she couldn't escape.

"Don't worry, love. I'm far more interested in sucking on that sweet little clit of yours until you can't come anymore."

Her eyes widened, and he caught the scent of her arousal. Unable to resist, he buried his face in her neck and licked the tender skin. She shivered but she wasn't pulling away from him, and triumph roared through him.

Then his datapad chimed, and she jumped and stepped back. *Fuck. Now what?*

Cursing under his breath, he strode over and flipped the switch.

"What is it?" he snapped impatiently.

"You asked us to search the monitors for any unidentified flying objects entering the atmosphere," Captain Nargan said patiently.

Lily gasped and came over to join him, pressing against his side. He automatically put his arm around her slender shoulders.

"Yes?"

"We only have a record of one such object. Since there was no attempt to control its destination, or to slow its entry, we assumed that it was a meteorite."

His eyes closed as he seethed. Those bastard slavers hadn't even bothered to put her in an escape pod with any type of working controls. If he ever got his hands on them, he would tear them limb from limb with his bare claws.

"Were there any others?" Lily demanded anxiously, and he relayed the question to Captain Nargan.

"No, sir. No other unidentified objects, either controlled or not."

He felt Lily sag against his side and pulled her against his chest.

"Will you send the same inquiry to Yangu? And perhaps Mafana?" The inhabitants of the ocean world did not associate frequently with the other planets in their system, but they remained on civil terms.

"Yes, sir." There was a moment's hesitation. "Hudomo asked me to remind you that a representative from House Bishar is scheduled to arrive today." Nargan cleared his throat, obviously uncomfortable with his role as intermediary. Leotra couldn't blame him. He should have realized that ordering Hudomo not to disturb him was bound to backfire.

"Very well. Have Hudomo send the information to my datapad."

"Yes, sir." Captain Nargan hung up without any further comment, which was one of the reasons that Leotra preferred using the Bukharans as his personal guards instead of his own species. Most Tajiri males would have been unable to resist expressing their curiosity about his unusual attempt to sequester himself. And he was quite sure that word of Lily's presence in his quarters had already spread.

"What are those other places you asked about?" Lily demanded. He could see the strain on her face and feel the tension in her shoulders.

"They are the other two planets in this solar system. Mafana is an ocean world inhabited by a different species. Yangu is the Tajiri home world and where I usually reside."

"You don't live here?"

"No, I come here to get away and go hunting. Although I never expected to capture such a delightful prey."

"You didn't capture me," she said crossly, but as he hoped, some of the despair on her face was replaced by annoyance.

"And yet you're here."

"Because you tricked me."

"I have never lied to you, Lily."

"You didn't tell me the entire truth either."

Her blue eyes snapped blue fire at him, and he winced. But then she sighed. "Although I guess if all females fawn over you like that servant, it makes a little more sense."

He was about to tell her that the servant's advances had been extremely mild compared to some of the other attempts that had been made to entice him, but decided that she probably wouldn't appreciate the information. At least, he hoped that she would be as displeased by them as she had been by the earlier female.

"Do you think you'll be able to find out anything about the other pods?" she asked hopefully, returning to the previous subject.

"I don't know," he said honestly. "The Mafana have many competing Houses, although they usually present a unified face to outsiders. I believe they will cooperate eventually, but there may be some internal discussions first."

"And what about your planet, Yangu?"

He sighed. "I'm afraid that might be a little more difficult. It is a heavily populated world with a lot of space traffic. The merchant houses do not willingly divulge information unless they see the chance of profit."

He hated to see the sorrow in her eyes and tugged her back into his arms.

"I promise that I will do everything I can to find out."

"Thank you." Her voice was muffled against his chest, but it sounded suspiciously watery. The thought of her crying made him want to stab something, but his anger wouldn't relieve her suffering. Perhaps it would be better to distract her.

He reached down and slid his hand under the hem of the shirt she was wearing so he could squeeze her luscious little ass. He heard her breath catch and smiled with satisfaction.

"You're going to have to choose an outfit now," he whispered.

"What do you mean?" She gave him a suspicious glare—which he much preferred over her previous sorrow.

"You don't want to meet the representative of House Bishar wearing only my shirt, do you?"

"I don't want to meet him at all."

"I don't particularly want to meet him either, but unfortunately it's necessary. And of course, you will accompany me."

Her skin was so soft beneath his hand. His shaft was already hard as he let his thumb slide over to tease the crevice between her cheeks.

"I will do nothing of the kind. Why should I?"

"Because you are my ma—my female."

She gave that adorable little growl again, and he hardened even further.

"No, I'm not."

Why did her defiance make him so hard? He wanted to kiss her until she melted against him, then carry her off to the bedroom and make her come until she could no longer deny that she was his.

But unfortunately, such pleasures will have to wait, he thought as his datapad pinged again. He needed to review the scheduled events and any background information that the efficient Hudomo would have provided.

But before he let her go, he dipped further between her legs and found the evidence of her body's response. He circled his thumb in the slick heat, then teased the sensitive pucker of her bottom hole before pulling away.

Her eyes glared at him, but her cheeks were flushed and her nipples thrusting against the fabric of her shirt. She was most definitely his.

CHAPTER FOURTEEN

When Leo reappeared at the entrance to the sitting room, Lily's mouth went dry. Even though he had admitted the necessity of meeting with the representative, he hadn't been in a hurry to leave her. Since he had dismissed the obnoxious female, he insisted on serving her food himself. She still wasn't sure exactly what she had eaten, but the majority of it had been delicious and he had quickly noted her preferences.

Even after they ate, he had remained with her, answering her questions about not only the planets that made up his solar system, but the larger political landscape of the Kaisarian Empire.

"You really have an Emperor?"

"Of course. Why does that surprise you?"

"It just seems very... archaic."

He shrugged. "There are a number of different systems of government in the Empire. Mafana also has a primarily hereditary ruling class—although they have been known to recognize new Houses if the families have sufficient wealth."

"What about Yangu?"

"We have a ruling Council, made up of representatives from the top one thousand merchant houses."

"Who decides which Houses are the top?"

"Top is determined purely by financial standing."

"So if you're poor, you have no say in the matter?"

"Your House speaks for you," he assured her. "And it's always possible to improve one's station. My grandfather started with one small mine and built an empire. He had a seat on the Council before his fortieth birthday."

The pride in his voice was obvious, and she wondered again when he had lost his grandfather, but before she could ask, he started asking her about the government on Earth. They spent most of the afternoon talking, and although she could see the heat in his eyes, he didn't lay another finger on her. She told herself she wasn't disappointed.

At last, he sighed and went to prepare for his meeting.

When he returned, the leather loincloth had been replaced by dark blue pants tucked into gold knee-high boots and fastened with a heavy gold belt. Over them he wore a long, sleeveless robe that opened over his chest. The dark blue material matched his eyes and was accented by intricate gold embroidery on each side of the opening. He looked magnificent and imposing, except…

"What did you do to your hair?" she blurted out.

The wild mane he had sported in the jungle had disappeared, replaced by elaborate curls that reminded her of the lead singer of some '80s hair band. It didn't make him less handsome—nothing could do that—but he didn't look like her Leo anymore.

No, he's not mine. Even if it felt as if he was.

"My mane? This is the latest style. You do not like it?" He looked more curious than offended.

She shook her head. "Not really. It's too... formal."

He stalked towards her. "Then perhaps you should make it less formal."

When he bent his head down, she swallowed, but she put her hands in his mane, running her fingers through the stiff curls until they were loose and wild around his face again. He purred softly beneath her touch and she had the sudden impulse to forget about his betrayal and just tug him closer. Instead, she took a step back.

The resulting look was a little bit wild, a little bit dangerous, and it made her heart skip a beat.

"There. That's better."

She did her best to keep her voice neutral, but she suspected she wasn't entirely successful. His eyes were fixed on her face.

"You should come with me."

She licked her lips, almost tempted. "It's too late."

"No, it's not. He'll wait."

The unconscious arrogance in his voice made her frown and the impulse to accompany him disappeared. She shook her head.

"I'd rather stay here."

He studied her face and she wondered if he was going to try and bully her into going.

"Very well," he said instead, then bent down to brush his lips against hers. "But I will miss you."

Then he was gone in a swirl of robes, leaving her staring after him, her fingers pressed to her mouth. Dammit. Why did he have to be so sweet sometimes?

She was still staring at the door when there was a quiet knock and another female servant slipped inside. Like the previous female, she was dressed in loose white pants gathered at the ankles and a matching short, sleeveless top. Unlike the other female, she looked nervous, her eyes fastened on the floor.

"Master Leotra sent me to accompany you," she whispered, her voice barely audible.

Lily scowled at the servant. Didn't he trust her by herself? Did he think she was going to flee back to the jungle? Part of her was almost tempted, but her previous experiences hadn't exactly made her confident about her chances of survival.

"I don't need company," she snapped.

"Yes, Mistress." The female seemed to shrink, her hand hovering nervously over the door control. "I-I'm sorry if I offended you."

Lily sighed. "You didn't offend me. I suppose you might as well come in."

"Thank you, Mistress." The female bobbed her head, then gave her a shy smile, and Lily realized she was just a girl.

"What's your name?"

"I'm Mata."

"Come and have a seat, Mata. You can give me your perspective on House Situni."

"Me, Mistress?"

"Yes. I suspect you might not see things the way Leo does."

Mata perched nervously on the edge of a cushion as Lily started questioning her but to her surprise, the girl didn't seem bothered by the social inequities. Even allowing for her natural reticence, she seemed both devoted to the interests of the House and proud of their standing.

"Master Leotra and his grandfather, Master Kubwan, have been very good to us."

"Doesn't he have a father? What about him?"

A shadow crossed the girl's face, and she looked down at her hands. "I haven't met him. My father doesn't allow me on house duty while he is here."

Interesting. Especially in light of Leo's previous comment about his father expecting servants to be accommodating. But since Mata obviously didn't want to discuss it, Lily changed the subject to the girl's family. Both of her parents worked at the lodge, and Mata had been born here on Sayari. Although she mentioned visiting Yangu wistfully, she seemed quite happy with her life and was soon chatting cheerfully.

As night fell, Mata ordered food for Lily—which Lily insisted she share—and then shyly suggested a movie. It turned out to be a sweeping historical epic with a ridiculously over-the-top hero, but the girl was enthralled and Lily found it surprisingly enjoyable. Once it was over, she sent a yawning Mata off to bed.

"But I should wait until Master Leotra returns," the girl protested.

"I'm just going to bed. You don't need to sit here and watch me sleep."

"Yes, Mistress."

As Mata moved to the door, a sudden thought struck Lily. Leo seemed determined to provide her with a female companion, and she would much rather have Mata than someone like the horrible female who had been there earlier.

"Are you coming back tomorrow, Mata?"

"Me? I'm not sure. There are many servants available."

"But I don't want someone else. I want you to come back."

Mata's sweet smile lit up her face, then she bobbed her head again. "Yes, Mistress."

Silence descended after the girl departed, and Lily wondered if she should have let her stay after all. *I'm quite capable of being on my own*, she reminded herself as she wandered into the bedroom. The massive bed was raised on a slight dais and draped with midnight blue curtains. Despite the overstated opulence, it looked extremely comfortable and she was tempted to climb in. But if Leo returned and found her in bed, he would assume she was waiting for him.

Aren't you? a traitorous voice whispered. Maybe, but she wasn't ready to just fall back into bed with him. Instead she returned to the sitting area and curled up on the couch, determined to wait up for him.

By the time Leotra could escape the formal dinner without unforgivable insult, he was tired and annoyed. He'd only been away from Yangu for two weeks, but he had already forgotten how tedious he found the interplay of communication. Nothing was ever said outright. Instead, a barbed sting would be hidden behind smiling words or a negotiation veiled in casual conversation.

It had taken him most of the lengthy and extravagant meal to discover exactly why Wakala, the representative of House Bishar, had come to Sayari. Hidden in the gentle flow of conversation was a proposal that Leotra take the daughter of the House as his mate. It was not, of course, the first time that such an alliance had been proposed. He was quite capable of maneuvering the conversation in such a way that the representative would have no real indication of his desire to accept or refuse. But somehow, tonight, he couldn't be bothered. The elaborate meal sat heavy in his stomach, the conditioned air was too cold, and the natural fragrance of the jungle had been replaced by cloyingly sweet artificial scents.

"No," he said abruptly, interrupting Wakala's latest conversational gambit.

"I'm sorry, Master Leotra?"

"I will be unable to form an alliance with House Bishar. Although I thank you for the gracious offer," he added as politely as possible.

Wakala gaped at him, and Leotra almost smiled. Had anyone ever been so blunt with the other male before?

"I-I don't understand. I never said—"

"I know you didn't. But we both know that was your intention. I'm simply telling you that you're wasting your time. I have made... arrangements elsewhere."

"I was not informed," Wakala said stiffly.

"It is a very recent development. We have not yet made the announcement, but since our Houses are so closely allied, I wanted to share the news with you."

As he hoped, Wakala relaxed somewhat. House Bishar was smaller and had less resources, but they were a good business partner and he did not want to damage the relationship with his bluntness.

"I understand, Master Leotra. And now I also understand why I was unable to set up a meeting with you previously."

Leotra frowned. He'd heard nothing of any request for a meeting. "Is that why you felt it necessary to come to Sayari to meet with me?"

"Why, yes. I have been trying to arrange a meeting for several months, but I was always informed that you were unavailable. Thank you for your candor."

"You are most welcome. I apologize that you were not informed previously. And I hope that I can rely on your discretion until the official announcement is made?"

Wakala quickly assured him of his silence, but Leotra knew it was unlikely. Gossip was the lifeblood of communication on Yangu.

What possessed me to be so blunt? he wondered as he returned to his quarters. Despite their encounter the previous night, Lily had certainly not been receptive to his claim today. But then again, she had obviously not appreciated the female servant's interest in him. Perhaps this could work out to his advantage after all.

He was smiling as he opened the door to his sitting area, but his smile vanished at the sight of Lily asleep on the couch. *Unacceptable.* His female belonged in his bed.

CHAPTER FIFTEEN

Lily woke up as Leo scooped her up and headed for the bedroom.

"What are you doing?" she asked, still half-asleep.

"Taking you to my bed. Where you belong," he growled.

He sounded annoyed, and she hid a smile. "I'm just fine on the couch."

"No, you are not. You will sleep in my—*our*—bed."

"But what if I don't want to sleep with you?" She kept her voice light, but she really wanted to know if he thought he was going to make her sleep with him.

"Why wouldn't you? Don't you know how many females have wanted to share my bed?"

The arrogant tone was back, and she scowled at him. "Then go find one of them."

"I don't want one of them. I want you."

They stared at each other, and then he sighed. "Fine. If you do not want me in the bed with you then I will sleep on the couch. But you will sleep here."

She was almost tempted to take him up on his offer, but it

was a ridiculously large bed—and if he was on the couch, he would be at the mercy of another one of those predatory female servants.

"I guess you might as well sleep here too. But no funny business," she added when he gave her a satisfied smile.

"Funny business?"

"You know. Sex."

He raised an eyebrow. "I assure you, I take that very seriously."

Her body gave an involuntary shiver as she remembered just how seriously, but she refused to acknowledge it. "I mean you stay on your side of the bed and I'll stay on mine."

"If that is what you wish."

He settled her between the sheets, then turned away and began stripping off his clothes.

"What - what are you doing?"

"I am preparing for bed, of course. I do not usually wear clothing to bed."

By the time he finished speaking and turned back to her, he was naked. Her mouth went dry at the expanse of golden fur-covered muscles and the heavy weight of his cock hanging against his thigh. It flexed under her gaze, and she hastily looked away.

"Your side of the bed," she reminded him.

"If you insist." He shrugged, massive shoulders rolling, then climbed into the other side of the bed.

The mattress was so large that she didn't even feel it move under his weight. The lights slowly dimmed, leaving the room in darkness except for the faint glow of the moonlight through the uncovered windows. It felt strange seeing the shadow of the leaves moving outside, but not hearing the sounds that she had started to recognize and to smell nothing but the faint remnant of the scented bath soaps.

The bed cradled her body, incredibly soft, but also supporting her perfectly. The cool, silky sheets caressed her skin. She should have fallen asleep immediately. Instead, she started to worry. To worry about her friends, of course, but also about her future and about the male on the other side of the bed. Even though they weren't touching, she could feel his presence.

Why did everything feel so complicated all of a sudden? When they were out in the jungle, it had seemed so much simpler. But now it was clear that he was a rich and probably powerful male. Her differences might amuse him now, but how long would that last? Back on Earth, she would already have been making plans to move on. Her legs twitched restlessly, as if she was preparing to run.

"What's bothering you, love?" Leo's voice was a deep rumble in the quiet room.

"Nothing."

"I should have brought some moni sap with me. You are not being truthful." He must have rolled over because she could suddenly feel his heat next to her, even though he still wasn't touching her. "Of course, there are other ways to get you to tell me the truth…"

"What do you mean?"

A huge hand skated across her ass so quickly that it only left a brief impression of warmth on her suddenly over sensitive skin.

"Perhaps I should spank you for lying to me."

Arousal washed over her so quickly that she actually felt the rush of heat between her thighs.

"You wouldn't!"

"Wouldn't I?" An electric tension hummed between, and then he sighed. "Perhaps not. At least not until I am sure that you trust me."

"I don't trust anyone." Somehow it was easier to make the admission in the shadowy darkness.

"I know. But for tonight, pretend that you do and let me hold you." His arm came around her, and he tucked her against his side. He purred against her ear. "You sleep well in my arms."

He only had a loose hold on her, and she was quite sure she could pull away from him... if she wanted to move. But he was big and warm and his scent wrapped around her, already comforting and familiar. What would it hurt to sleep together?

His warmth seeped into her muscles, and the tension started to dissipate. She found herself nestling closer as sleep finally came.

LEOTRA SMILED AS LILY SETTLED DOWN AND FELL ASLEEP. She felt so perfect in his arms. The way a mate should feel. It was an old-fashioned notion. These days most matings were arranged for political or financial advantage, but his feelings for Lily came from a deeper, more primal place.

Up until now, he had not considered the future, but Wakala's proposal had made him realize that he couldn't ignore it. Of course, it was always possible that he could claim an official mate and still keep Lily as his concubine. It was certainly not uncommon in Tajiri society, but every atom of his body rebelled against the idea. He refused to set her aside, even as a surface gesture.

But would she commit to him in return? He was unusually uncertain. He knew she wanted him, despite her denials, and he suspected that her feelings went even deeper, but he didn't know if she was prepared to admit them to herself, let alone to him. Based on what she had told him, males had never treated her well. The fact that he hadn't revealed the truth about himself to her immediately hadn't helped.

What he needed was time to convince her—which meant she had to remain at his side. As close to his side as if they were in fact mates...

The idea sprang full-fledged into his mind. What if he could convince her to pretend to be his mate? Such an arrangement would ensure that she remained with him. He would be able to not only protect her, but to provide her with the clothing and jewelry she deserved. It would also prevent any more awkward proposals from other Houses.

She mumbled something in her sleep, and he purred softly until she relaxed again.

Yes. This would be perfect. Now all he had to do was convince her. He was still considering how to accomplish that when he fell asleep.

When he woke the next morning, he found that she had practically crawled on top of him during the night. Her head was tucked under his chin, and her lush breasts were nestled against his chest. One leg was thrown over his, and her sweet little cunt was resting against his thigh. His cock throbbed impatiently. They had woken up in a similar position yesterday and he'd had no hesitation in pleasuring her, but he was no longer as sure.

She made a soft noise and wiggled against his leg. He stroked down her back to her ass, so bare and naked without a tail to impede his touch. Her soft flesh filled his hand as he prepared to move her back to his side. Instead, she arched against him, and he instinctively squeezed. He felt the resulting dampness against his thigh as she moaned and rolled her hips. His thumb slipped into the tempting crevice between her cheeks.

"Lily," he whispered, as he pressed lower, seeking the liquid heat slicking her thighs.

"Mmm?"

"Does your hot little cunt need me?" He teased her entrance, so small and tight it was almost impossible to believe that she had taken him.

"I..."

She lifted her head, and the uncertainty of her face was like an arrow to his chest.

"Your choice," he told her gently.

She started to sit up, and he moved his hand to her hip to help her lift herself free. Instead, she paused, still astride his thigh, her breasts quivering beneath his shirt. His cock ached, but he forced himself to wait patiently.

She rolled her hips again, and he felt another rush of heat against his thigh.

"My choice?"

"Always."

She bit her lip, then slowly pulled his shirt up over her head, leaving her naked and glowing in the morning light.

"Lick," she whispered, leaning forward so that her tempting nipples hovered just above his mouth.

He obeyed immediately, groaning with pleasure as he curled his tongue around a tight little peak. She rocked back and forth on his thigh and he started to pull the tantalizing morsel into his mouth. She immediately pulled back.

"I only said lick."

"You are a cruel female," he protested but he suddenly realized that she was testing him. "What would you like me to do next? Lick your delicious little clit? Bury my tongue in your hot cunt?"

More wetness flooded his thigh.

"Lick me," she whispered.

"Where?"

"My—my clit."

He promptly flipped her over on her back and buried his face between her legs. His tongue circled the swollen button, as he forced himself to simply lick the delicious nub. Her hips lifted restlessly.

"Do you want more, love? Do you want my finger filling you? Or do you want two stretching you?"

"Yes," she gasped.

"One? Two? More?"

"Two! While you suck my clit."

He obeyed immediately, sucking her clit into his mouth as he plunged two fingers into her tight channel. Her body bowed upwards, and she cried out his name as she clenched around him with sharp little pulses. His cock was so hard he felt as if it would drill through the mattress, but he forced himself to wait until her body softened and she gave a contented little sigh.

Lifting up over her, he smiled down at her dazed face. His cock flexed against the silky heat between her thighs, but he resisted the urge to thrust into her sweet cunt.

"Was that enough, love? Or do you want more?"

CHAPTER SIXTEEN

Lily's eyes opened, still heavy with pleasure, but Leotra could see the hint of uncertainty. Very well. He was a patient hunter. He could wait.

He pressed a quick kiss to her lips, then rolled to his feet, ignoring his aching cock.

"Come. It is time to be about our day."

She looked so shocked he almost laughed. Shocked and... disappointed? Her eyes dropped to his cock, and that provocative little tongue swept across her lips.

"What about you?"

"Are you offering to relieve my suffering?" He deliberately kept his tone light, and her eyes snapped back up to his.

"Suffering?"

"Very much so." He took his shaft in his hand and gave it a long, exaggerated stroke. "I am aching for you."

Her eyes followed the movement and he repeated it. He would much rather have had her cunt or her mouth or her hand on him, but if all he could get was her gaze, he would take it.

"Are you offering?"

"I... No." She didn't sound convinced, but he didn't press her.

"Then I will attempt to relieve myself in the shower."

He turned away, letting his tail lash behind him as he left the room and headed for the shower. A Tajiri female would have recognized it as an invitation, but he didn't expect Lily to respond. Which was why his eyes flew open in shock as a small, soft hand tried to close around him a few moments later.

"What are you doing?"

She gave him an innocent look totally at odds with the sensuous way she was squeezing his shaft.

"Don't you know?"

He groaned, trying to gather the thoughts that had scattered at her touch, at the sight of her pink and naked and glowing in the stream of water. She gave him a smug look and stroked him again, twisting her hand slightly as she reached the head of his cock. Electricity streaked down his spine so quickly that he felt light-headed. He was on the verge of exploding from her touch like an untried youth.

"You... you don't have to touch me." *But gods, please don't stop.*

"Maybe I just wanted to pay you back," she said lightly.

He growled and clamped his hand down over hers. "You do not need to pay me. I will happily pleasure your hot little cunt whenever you ask."

Her eyes widened and even through the fall of water he caught the scent of her arousal.

"I... I didn't mean it like that."

"You only ever need to touch me because you want to. Do you want to?"

"Yes."

He tightened his hand around hers and dragged those small, soft fingers down the length of his shaft. His barbs flexed, stirring restlessly. Her other hand reached lower, cupping his testicles and squeezing gently. He growled, using his free hand to grab her ass and pull her closer.

"I'm not going to last long," he warned her.

"Good. I like knowing I make you as crazy as you make me." Her voice was breathless, her face determined, as she stroked harder, twisting and pulling with a firm pressure that he was helpless to resist.

His roar echoed through the room as he came in a thunderous explosion, his seed painting her stomach and breasts in jets of creamy gold. She never faltered, only easing her grip until it was a soothing caress as he sagged against the walls of the shower.

"Did I ease your suffering?" she teased, but her cheeks were flushed and her nipples rosy little peaks.

"Temporarily."

A golden drop had pearled on her nipple and he swiped it off with his thumb as she shuddered. He lifted it to her mouth and she opened immediately.

"Mmm."

The erotic sight sent a fresh wave of desire through his body, but he did his best to ignore it as he reluctantly washed his seed from her body. She purred under his hands almost like a Tajiri female. By the time he finished washing her, he was fully, achingly erect once more.

"I guess temporarily was right," she murmured, licking her lips as she looked down at his cock. "Do you need more... relief?"

He groaned, but forced himself to shake his head.

"Be on your way, temptress. There are things to be done." He turned her towards the shower door and lightly smacked her ass.

He saw the way she shivered, saw the way she hesitated,

and he wanted nothing more than to pull her back against him and give her what her body so clearly wanted. But he had promised to help find her friends, and he wasn't quite sure her mind was as willing as her body. He let her go.

Fighting the impulse to stay with Leo, Lily reluctantly left him in the shower and went to pick out another one of his shirts to wear. *Why did I join him in the first place?* she wondered. Despite her teasing words, it wasn't just because he had made her come so thoroughly.

Maybe sleeping together wasn't a good idea. As comforting as it had been, it had left her feeling safe and protected in a way that she knew from experience was only an illusion. And yet, when she woke up this morning, she had been happy to be wrapped in his arms.

Pulling on his shirt, she wandered out to the sitting room just as Mata entered pushing a small cart heaped with food.

"Good morning, Mistress. Would you like to break your fast in here, or would you prefer to use the dining room?"

"I'm not really dressed to go wandering around the place," she said dryly, gesturing to her makeshift outfit.

"Oh no. I meant in Master Leotra's personal dining room."

"He has a personal dining room?"

Mata nodded and opened a panel concealed in the wall to reveal a room almost as large as Lily's entire apartment. The massive wooden table was formed from a single slab of one of the giant trees and could easily have accommodated a dozen people.

"This is small?" she muttered.

The indication of his immense wealth suddenly seemed oppressive, and she walked over to the long windows, looking longingly at the jungle. There was a much smaller table on the balcony, along with some comfortable padded chairs. "Can we eat outside instead?"

Mata looked surprised, but she bobbed her head willingly and pushed the cart onto the balcony. The soft chitter of insects and the rich scents of the jungle felt familiar, and Lily found herself relaxing again. She took a deep breath, then went to help Mata set out the food despite the girl's protests.

"Don't be silly. I've been a waitress on more than one occasion."

"Really?"

Lily laughed at Mata's obvious shock. "Of course. I was not always as you see me now."

Mata's eyes flicked to her, and then she ducked her head. "Perhaps you would like me to help you dress after your meal?"

"Now why do I think that's just a nice way of telling me that I need to wear something more respectable?"

"Oh, no, Mistress. I just wasn't sure if you were familiar with our clothing styles."

"You are very tactful, Mata. I suppose it would be nice to have something else to wear—I just didn't want something left behind by one of Leo's other females."

Mata bit her lip. "Master Leotra has never brought another female here."

"Really?"

"Yes, really." Leo's deep voice made them both jump guiltily. He was standing in the doorway behind them, clad only in a pair of long loose pants, his mane still damp from the shower, and her heart skipped a beat.

"I'm so sorry, Master Leotra," Mata said quickly. "I didn't mean to gossip."

Leo waved a hand as he strolled over and put his arm around Lily. "I assigned you to Mistress Lily. You are free to answer any questions she wishes to ask you."

"Yes, sir."

"I did tell you that they didn't belong to another female," Leo said, smiling down at her. "But since it appears to bother you so much, Mata, please arrange for Shona to attend us after our meal. In an hour, perhaps?"

"Yes, sir." Mata hovered uncertainly. "Would you like me to serve?"

"That won't be necessary. As Mistress Lily said, she is familiar with the act of service."

She glared up at him. "Were you eavesdropping?"

"Not intentionally, but I was using the communicator in the adjoining room to contact Captain Nargan."

Her annoyance vanished. "Is there any news?"

"I'm afraid not." He hesitated, then sat down and pulled her onto his lap as Mata disappeared. "But I think our search might be more successful if we were actually on Yangu. I could speak to the Mafanan ambassador personally, and I have some... connections to people who might be reluctant to talk to anyone in an official capacity."

"Leave here?" Based on what he had told her, there wouldn't be a jungle on Yangu—just more oppressive luxury. Her heart sank, but if he thought it was necessary to help find her friends, she wasn't going to argue. "If you think it will help."

"You don't seem enthusiastic, but Yangu has much to offer - from the finest restaurants to the most exclusive shops."

"Oh, yay," she said unenthusiastically.

"You are a very strange female."

She glared and tried to climb off his lap, but his arms tightened around her and he pulled her back down against him.

"It is very refreshing," he added, nuzzling her neck.

"Why are you so fond of my neck?"

"Because I can breathe in your scent while I mark you with

mine. It is where a Tajiri male always touches his mate."

"Mate?" Something about the way he purred the word set off an alarm in her brain.

"Ah, yes, about that. I believe the most expeditious course of action would be for you to pretend to be my mate."

"Why?"

"For three reasons. One, it will allow you to accompany me everywhere I go. Two, it removes any possibility that someone may consider you unprotected."

"I can protect myself."

"My love, I would like to remind you that you were unable to prevent your abduction. There are others who might attempt to follow in their footsteps."

An icy shiver ran down her spine. The last thing she wanted was to encounter more slavers.

"Is that really likely to happen?"

"Not as long as I live. But it will be easier for me to protect you as your mate."

"So this is just pretend?" she asked.

He hesitated for the briefest second. "It is the most appropriate choice."

"I suppose," she said finally.

He grinned down at her with a suspiciously triumphant look on his face.

"You said three reasons. What was the other one?"

"Why, to protect me, of course."

His expression turned solemn, but she could see the laughter dancing in his eyes.

"Protect you from what?"

"From all the females chasing after me. You will protect me, won't you?"

"Only if you're good." She let her hand brush across his cock. "Very, very good."

CHAPTER SEVENTEEN

Lily peered eagerly out the window of the spaceship as the surface of Yangu came into view. She hadn't been entirely sure what to expect after her experience on the slave ship, but the vessel that transported them from Sayari to Yangu bore a surprising resemblance to a luxury jet, at least on the inside. There was a comfortable seating area, a large bedroom, and a fully equipped bathroom. A kitchen and dining area and an area for the staff comprised the rest of the ship.

Mata smiled at her from her adjoining seat, her eyes wide with excitement. When Leo had ordered the girl to accompany them, Lily had been annoyed at his peremptory behavior. However, when she took Mata aside and asked her, the girl had been thrilled at the idea of the journey.

The morning had disappeared in a whirlwind of activity. Shona, the seamstress Leo had sent for, had been unable to produce new clothing before they left, but she had adapted a few of the outfits Leo had previously chosen. Lily still wasn't enthusiastic about wearing someone else's clothes, but if they didn't belong to one of Leo's mistresses, she could live with them. He had also promised to take her shopping, although the prospect did not thrill her.

While the alterations were in progress, Leo had met with the male he'd had dinner with the night before to apologize for his abrupt departure. As soon as her clothes were ready, he'd led her to a concealed landing area, the ultra-modern space at complete odds to the surrounding jungle. His personal guard accompanied them, huge bull-like males complete with sweeping horns. She vaguely remembered that two of them had been on the hovercraft that picked them up from the jungle, but at the time she'd been too upset by Leo's betrayal to pay much attention.

Now she found their size and alien features more intimidating than she expected, but she did her best not to show her reaction as Leo introduced her to their leader.

"Lily, this is Captain Nargan."

"You're the one trying to find my friends. Thank you so much."

The big male looked a little surprised, but he bowed politely.

"Mistress Lily is my mate. You will protect her at all costs, do you understand?"

"Yes, Master Leotra."

This time, he didn't look surprised and Lily wondered why not. Had Leo already spread the word about their fake relationship? She still wasn't entirely sure how she felt about the prospect, but she couldn't deny that she felt safer with Leo—and his guards—at her side.

A personal spaceship wasn't bad either, she thought, as Kalima came into view. The immense capital city sprawled towards the horizon. The sun had just set, leaving a pale lavender glow that highlighted the astonishing variety of buildings rising into the air above the city. Lights had come on below to reveal an intricate network of streets and smaller buildings. In addition to the traffic at ground level, small vessels darted between the skyscrapers. Some of the towers were so tall and slender it seemed impossible that they would be able to stand, and her heart sank as they headed for one of the tallest.

"Where are we going?" she asked nervously.

"Situni Tower. It belongs to my family. Our businesses are run from there, and I have an apartment at the top."

A few minutes later, the ship came to a halt, hovering near the top of a slender navy tower. She dutifully followed Leo to the exit, clenching her fists to hide their trembling. The doors opened to reveal a walkway leading from the ship to the building. The floor was opaque, but the curved walls were made from a clear substance, meaning she could see the city surrounding them.

Leo was a step in front of her, issuing instructions to Captain Nargan, and she forced herself to follow him. One step, then another, and then she made the fatal mistake of looking down. The ground was far, far below in a dizzying swirl of lights. Vertigo swept over her, and she swayed, unable to move.

"Lily! What's wrong?"

She could hear Leo's voice, but she could also feel the tunnel quivering from the wind at this altitude. Her lips felt numb.

"Talk to me, love." Leo's arms closed around her, warm and comforting.

"S-So high," she managed to stutter.

She heard him give a muttered curse, and he swept her up into his arms. She buried her face in his neck, ashamed of her fear but unable to face the trip.

"We are inside now," he said soothingly a moment later, but

she still felt as if everything was swaying. Her arms tightened around his neck.

"Mata, go to the kitchen and ask the chef for a glass of Foldaran brandy. A large one," he ordered.

"You should say please," she muttered.

His laugh reverberated soothingly against her body.

"You must be feeling better if you're bossing me around again."

"You're the bossy one."

"Very bossy," he agreed softly, dipping his head to growl the words into her ear. A much more pleasant shiver went through her body.

He seemed perfectly content just to stand and hold her, but a moment later she heard Mata's voice and then Leo pressed a glass against her lips. She took a sip and almost choked at the burn of alcohol. The initial heat faded quickly, leaving a pleasant smoky aftertaste and a trickle of warmth all the way down to her stomach. She licked her lips and took another sip.

"What did you say this was?"

"Foldaran brandy."

"It's very good."

"It should be. It's older than I am." He smiled down at her. "That's better. The color is coming back to your cheeks."

"I feel better," she admitted, her cheeks heating. "I'm sorry I reacted that way."

"Don't be silly. Many people are not comfortable with the sky bridges. Do you want to walk, or would you like me to carry you?"

"I can walk."

"What a shame," he whispered as he sat her down. "I enjoy having your soft little body in my arms."

Doing her best not to blush, she looked around instead. Everyone had disappeared except for Mata. The girl gave her a sympathetic smile, then whisked herself out of sight. The doors that must have led to the ship were thankfully closed, and they were in a wide corridor. The wall on one side was lined with a collection of large abstract paintings. On the other side, a glass wall showcased an array of sleek, expensive-looking vehicles. The white stone flooring in the corridor extended seamlessly into the huge space.

"Are those yours?"

He actually looked a little embarrassed. "I am fond of vehicles."

"Do you actually drive them?" she asked, looking at the pristine area.

"Oh, yes. And I can't wait to take you for a ride."

"I think you're already doing that," she muttered, and he laughed as he dropped his arm around her shoulder and urged her along the hallway.

At the far end, a set of shallow stone steps led upwards. More art ornamented the staircase, this time with sculptures set on pedestals.

"Did you pick out the art pieces?" she asked, stopping to admire a sinuous metal sculpture.

"Some of it. My grandfather started the collection, and I have added to it."

"What about your father?" She had already noticed that he never mentioned him.

He shook his head, his mouth twisting. "He tends to acquire pieces based solely on their cost. I don't have any of them here. Do you like this one?"

"I do."

"This is one I selected. It's called The Lovers. You see, this is the female, with her male behind her."

He traced the line with his finger as he spoke, and she could clearly envision their bodies pressed together the same way. A rush of heat swept over her, but she told herself that it was the lingering effects of the brandy.

"Is that why you chose it?"

"I chose it because the artist is extremely talented. But I enjoy sensual objects." His finger traveled lightly down her back and across her ass in the exact same way it had traveled across the statue. Before she could decide how to react, he put his arm back around her shoulders and urged her onwards.

The enormous apartment occupied the top four levels of the tower. The garage and staff quarters were on the lowest level. The kitchens and more staff quarters occupied the second level, along with an enormous dining room with glass walls on three sides. She found that looking out over the city didn't bother her as much as looking down, and fortunately, her vertigo didn't reappear. The third level contained more entertaining spaces, along with Leo's study and several guest bedrooms.

The top level was the most impressive. A glass-walled pavilion containing Leo's bedroom, bath, and sitting area stood in the center of an enormous roof deck filled with lush vegetation. The air was surprisingly still, and she realized that more glass walls blocked the wind but they were almost invisible behind the assortment of plants. A swimming pool with an infinity edge was perched along one side of the deck, underwater lights turning the water dark and mysterious under the night sky.

"This is beautiful," she breathed.

"It's my favorite place, but it is far more beautiful with you here."

She raised a skeptical eyebrow and turned to tease him about his corny lines, but the expression on his face took her breath away. He looked so sincere. Time hung suspended between them, the noise of the city muted and far away, and then he cleared his throat and looked away.

"I thought perhaps we would have dinner at Hawa Pendez. It is the most exclusive restaurant in Kalima."

The prospect did not appeal to her in the least, and she sighed. "Do we have to?"

"You don't wish to accompany me?"

"It's been a long day. Several long days. Couldn't we just stay here? Maybe go for a swim?"

He frowned, and she wondered if she had offended him.

"You would rather stay here with me than have dinner at the finest restaurant in the city?"

"Isn't that what I just said?" *Why does he look so surprised?*

"Are all human females like you?" he asked slowly.

"Of course not. Are all Tajiri males like you?"

He looked offended, then laughed. "An excellent point. I would be quite happy to remain here with you. Although..."

His eyes traveled down her body with the heat that sent a corresponding response through her.

"Yes?"

"I don't have any swimming apparel." His voice had turned low and rough.

"I imagine we can work something out." She gave him a teasing smile and let her fingers brush very lightly across his erect shaft as she headed back to the pavilion.

Leo went off to order dinner and check on some business matters, and Mata came to join her. She hovered uncertainly at the entrance to the bedroom as Lily explored. Another enormous bed, this one draped in white, but there was very little other furniture to detract from the stunning surroundings and she liked the simplicity of the space.

"Are you going out tonight, Mistress?"

"No, thank goodness." Something that looked like disappointment flickered across Mata's face, and Lily gave her a thoughtful look. "Why do you ask?"

Mata's tail twitched nervously. "I just wanted to know if I should be ready to serve you."

Which meant that she would need to stay in the apartment in case Lily wanted her. The light dawned as she remembered the girl's excitement about the trip.

"I get it. You want to go and explore, and you can't if you're hanging around here waiting on me."

"Oh, no, Mistress. I'm happy to stay here."

"Don't be silly." In her first years of traveling with the band, she'd always enjoyed exploring new cities. But Mata seemed very innocent. She hesitated for a minute, then picked up the datapad and pressed the button Leo had shown her.

"Yes, Mistress Lily?" Nargan's deep voice answered immediately.

"Captain Nargan, Mata wishes to see some of the city." She ignored the girl's gasp.

"Mata?" he repeated.

"Yes, my... maid."

"I know who she is, Mistress."

"She's never been to Kalima before. Do you have a guard who could accompany her?"

"You want a guard to accompany a maid?"

"Yes. Is that a problem?"

"Not at all. You just surprised me." But he sounded contemplative rather than disapproving. "I will send someone up immediately."

"Someone trustworthy."

"All of my males are trustworthy," he replied coldly.

"Yes, of course. I didn't mean to suggest otherwise. It's just that she's very young."

"Don't worry. I have the perfect male."

Mata's eyes were as big as saucers as she ended the call. "Why did you do that?"

"Because I want you to go out and have fun and see the sights. But I don't want you to be in any danger."

"You are sure you don't need me?"

"Nope." She winked at the girl. "I have Leo to wait on me."

"Do you indeed?"

The deep voice made both of them jump, and she turned around to glare at him. "Quit sneaking up on me. And quit eavesdropping!"

"It's hardly my fault that I have excellent hearing." He prowled towards her, his tail lashing. "And just how do you propose I serve you?"

CHAPTER EIGHTEEN

Leotra regarded the pink in Lily's cheeks with great satisfaction—and the speculative gleam in her eyes pleased him even more.

"Mata is going out for the evening," she told him.

"Yes, I know."

Nargan had called to inform him, although interestingly enough, the captain had presented it as a fact rather than asking for permission. He seemed to have no hesitation in taking orders from Lily, and Leotra found that surprisingly satisfying.

"With your permission, of course, Master Leotra," Mata said quickly, her tail twitching anxiously.

"I would never dare to contradict Mistress Lily."

Lily snorted, and he saw Mata's lips twitch before she ducked her head and excused herself.

"You wouldn't dare to contradict me?" Lily asked, raising a delicate brow.

"Certainly not when it comes to Mata."

"Hmm... what if I wanted to spend all your money?"

He didn't even hesitate. "Go ahead. I doubt you would be able to do so, but you are welcome to try."

Her eyes widened, but she looked more dismayed than impressed. He wasn't surprised—he was quite sure she wasn't with him because of his wealth. Then her small blunt teeth closed down on her plump lower lip.

"What if I want to leave you?" she said quietly.

"No!" he roared, then did his best to soften his voice when she jumped. "I can't..." *Let you go.* "I mean, you would not be safe by yourself."

She tilted her head, an unreadable look on her face. "Am I safe with you?"

"Always." He stalked closer until their bodies were almost touching. "Let me be quite clear, love—you can spend my money, rearrange my household, and give whatever orders you desire to my staff. But I refuse to let you put yourself in danger."

"I'm not sure we have the same definition of danger," she said softly, then shook her head. The serious expression vanished as she smiled up at him. "Did you arrange for food? I'm hungry."

He wanted to press her, to find out what she was hiding, but decided that he would allow her to keep her secrets. For now.

"I came to tell you that it was ready."

He had arranged for the meal to be served on the terrace. Remembering how much she had enjoyed the night-blooming flowers on Sayari, he had also ordered candles to be scattered throughout the rooftop. Contentment filled him when she gasped in delight.

"This is so beautiful. It's almost like we're not in the city at all."

"Do you dislike the city?" he asked as he led her to a

lounging bench.

"Yes and no. I like the excitement and all the things to do, but somehow it makes you feel more alone when you're surrounded by all these other people."

An unexpected ache formed in his chest. She had described exactly the way he had begun to feel over the past few years as the unceasing round of social activities felt more and more meaningless.

"Neither of us is alone now," he said softly as he pulled her down on the lounge with him. Before she could respond, he reached for a tray of fruit and picked up a berry. "Open."

"You don't need to feed me."

He traced her lips with the berry, the deep red juice staining them. "You said you wanted me to serve you."

"I—"

As soon as she opened her mouth, he popped the fruit inside. She hummed with pleasure.

"I like that. What is it?"

"A tamu berry. You know, I've almost forgotten what they taste like."

"You should try it."

"I intend to."

He bent his head and kissed her. The juice flavored her mouth, but it wasn't as enticing as her natural sweetness.

"Delicious," he agreed when he finally forced himself to raise his head. The fragrance of her arousal mingled with the sweet scent of the berries. Her eyes were heavy-lidded with pleasure, and she licked her lips again as she looked up at him.

"Are you trying to seduce me, Master Situni?"

"Trying?" he asked in mock outrage. "You mean I'm not succeeding?"

"You may be succeeding a little too well."

He smiled and reached for another berry.

By the time he finished feeding her, juice stained her mouth and the taut points of her nipples. Her top had long since succumbed to his claws, and he could see the traces of his juice-stained hands and mouth on her neck and the soft skin of her stomach. The sight made him want to roar with pride. His female.

She followed his gaze. "You certainly made a mess."

"Yes," he agreed smugly.

"I'm afraid there's only one solution." She slipped out of his arms before he could prevent her. "A bath."

She shrugged out of the remains of her top and stepped out of her pants. For just a moment she paused, her body gleaming in the reflected lights of the city, lush and perfect. Then she turned and dove gracefully into the pool.

His own clothes disappeared almost as quickly—so quickly that he stumbled over the edge of the pool and entered the water with a huge splash. He surfaced, spluttering, and saw Lily's face bright with laughter.

"I guess even you can't be graceful all of the time."

No one ever dared to tease him the way she did, and he loved every minute of it. But he still growled and started stalking her. She squeaked and swam away, sliding through the water with surprising ease. He didn't catch up with her until she reached the infinity edge. She rested her arms on the ledge, looking out over the city.

"It looks beautiful from up here - as long as I don't look down."

"Do you have cities this size on your world?"

"There are some that might come close, but it's not the same."

"Do you miss it?" he asked softly.

"I think that's another yes and no question. I miss coffee and the sound of the ocean. I thought I'd found a place where I might want to stay for a while and I miss that possibility. But there wasn't anyone I was really close to." She turned to face him, and he automatically put his hands on her hips to support her. The darkness turned her eyes to deep blue pools. "Not even as close as we've become."

He could hear the question in her voice, but before he could respond, her seriousness vanished.

"Do you think I'm clean enough now?"

He lifted her higher so that her breasts were even with his mouth. "I'm afraid you need more attention. And I did promise to serve you."

He closed his mouth around one tempting little peak, the lingering coolness from the water an erotic contrast to the warmth of her skin. She gasped, and her hands tangled in his mane.

"More," she demanded as he licked and tugged, but he kept the pace slow, moving back and forth between the two buds until they were swollen and distended.

Then he carried her to the edge of the pool and laid her back on the smooth stone like an offering to the gods. He remained in the water as he spread her legs, her folds flushed pink and glistening from more than the pool water. The small pearl of flesh at the top of her slit was as red and tempting as one of the tamu berries, and he drew it deep into his mouth.

She arched her back and cried out, her voice lost in the night, and he growled approvingly.

"That's one."

"One?" She raised her head and looked down the length of her body at him.

He grinned, letting her see his fangs. "One climax. I intend to see how many I can serve your sweet little cunt."

Four. By the time she shattered the fourth time, his fingers buried deep in her hot little cunt and her even hotter ass, his fangs scraping delicately across the swollen pearl of her clit, her cry was little more than a hoarse whisper and her eyes fluttered closed even as she smiled up at him.

She barely moved as he climbed out of the pool and wrapped a towel around her, and she was asleep before he reached the bedroom. His cock throbbed, even though he had come twice in the pool just from the delicious taste and feel of her climaxes, but he smiled as he placed her between the sheets. She looked so perfect in his bed—already he couldn't imagine it without her.

As he started to join her, he noticed the light blinking on his data pad. Although he was tempted to ignore it, his responsibilities could not be abandoned forever. He took it into the other room, then scowled as he read the message.

His father demanded his presence for an event at the mansion the following night. If he knew his father, it would be another hedonistic gathering with secret deals being conducted in hidden corners. He usually avoided such parties, but perhaps it would be a good time to introduce Lily. They could make a brief appearance, just long enough to spread the news, and then he could bring her back here and have her all to himself once more.

He sent a brief acknowledgement, then returned to the bed. He scowled up at the ceiling, already dreading the following night, but then Lily rolled over and snuggled against his side and his annoyance disappeared. It would be a minor inconvenience, nothing else. The only thing that really mattered was the female in his arms.

CHAPTER NINETEEN

Mata was full of enthusiasm as she served Lily breakfast the next morning, chattering eagerly about all of the exciting things that Janob had shown her. A little concerned, Lily pushed her for more details, but it appeared that Janob had behaved like a perfect gentleman and taken Mata to the most innocuous places. Still, perhaps she would have Leo have a word with Nargan about the guard. And speaking of Leo...

"Where's Leo?" she asked as casually as possible, not wanting to admit how disappointed she had been when she woke up alone. Last night had been the most amazing experience. Even now the memory felt more like a surreal dream than something that had actually happened. Lying there with her legs dangling in the warm water while Leo drove her into climax after climax with his tongue and his hands and his exquisitely dirty mouth. The whole world seemed to narrow to the two of them, the glow of the city lights and the distant sounds of traffic only a faint backdrop. Waking by herself had made it even easier to imagine that it was just a dream.

"He's in his study, working," Mata said. "He told me not to disturb you."

Working? Hmm. She had convinced herself that he was one of the idle rich.

"What kind of work, exactly?"

"I don't really know. But the Situni corporation is involved in a lot of different businesses." Mata gave her a sly smile. "Why don't you go ask him?"

A flutter of anticipation bubbled up in Lily's stomach, and she smiled. "Only if you help me get dressed first."

Examining herself in the mirror a short time later, she couldn't help but smile. She thought this was the prettiest of the outfits that Shona had adjusted to fit her. Loose pants in a soft blue floral hung low on her hips—apparently most pants were cut that way in order to accommodate Tajiri tails. The fabric was almost sheer, but it was full enough to preserve her modesty. The matching top was tight across her breasts despite Shona's best efforts, and it rubbed pleasurably across her erect nipples. The top ended several inches above her belly button, leaving a wide expanse of her stomach visible. Pretty, yes, but definitely sexy and she started to have second thoughts.

"Maybe this isn't the best choice."

"Don't be silly," Mata said firmly, then ducked her head. "I'm sorry, Mistress."

"Don't worry about it. I'm trusting you to tell me the truth. And isn't that what Leo told you to do?"

Mata gave her a shy smile. "Yes, Mistress."

"Why don't you just call me Lily? At least when we're alone," she added when the girl's tail twitched nervously.

"Yes, Lily."

"That's better. And if you really think this outfit is okay, why don't you take me to Leo's study?"

Her doubts disappeared the moment she walked into the

room and Leo looked up and saw her. The hunger on his face sent a corresponding pulse of excitement to her clit.

"Am I interrupting? Mata said you were working."

"I'm afraid so, but your interruption is most welcome."

He held out his hand to her and when she went to join him, pulled her down on his lap and kissed her until she was breathless.

"Definitely welcome," he purred, tracing his claw delicately over her erect nipple as it thrust against the thin cloth of her top.

Despite the arousal flaring in her body, she managed to remember her question.

"What kind of work do you do?"

He sighed, and although he continued to play with her nipple, he looked suddenly distant.

"That's an excellent question. My father has a controlling interest in the company which means that I have very little actual authority. However, I do my best to check in periodically as well as monitor our various businesses to make sure that everything appears to be running smoothly." He tapped a claw on his desk. "For example, there is an import export company that was recently added to our portfolio and I'm having difficulty tracking down its inventory."

"And this is what you do with your time? When you're not chasing females through the jungle?"

He growled and rubbed his face against her neck. "I have only ever chased one female through the jungle. But no, I don't do this as often as I should. I find it... frustrating that I do not have the authority to make changes. Instead, I spend my time showing up at all of the latest hot spots and racing my vehicles and generally indulging myself," he added dryly.

"Do you include females in your list of indulgences?"

"I used to," he admitted, running his finger across her neck.

"But that became frustrating as well. I don't think any one of them were ever really interested in me, just my wealth."

Poor little rich boy. The thought rose unbidden to her mind, but she suspected he wouldn't appreciate it. Instead, she stroked her fingers through his mane and pulled his head back down for another kiss.

"Will you be working for much longer?" she asked when they finally separated, both of them breathing heavily.

"There's nothing that can't wait. I will ask Captain Nargan to look for more information about this company."

"Then whatever will we do?" She traced her finger down his chest.

"Not what I hope you are suggesting. I am going to take you shopping."

She sighed. Shopping had never been one of her favorite things. Her usual wardrobe consisted of jeans and vintage T-shirts with boots in the winter and sandals in the summer. She had some cute tops for the occasional date night and a nice collection of pretty underwear. But all of it was gone now and she would have to adjust.

"Is that because you don't like this outfit?"

"On the contrary, it is most delightful." He caught her nipple between his thumb and finger and tugged gently. "But we are going to an event tonight and you will need to be dressed differently."

"What kind of event?"

"A party my father is hosting at the Situni mansion." He didn't sound enthusiastic at the prospect.

"And we have to go?"

"I think it would be best. I will introduce you as my mate and have a few words with the Mafanan ambassador. Then we can make a quick exit and I can bring you back here and have you all to myself."

"That sounds much more pleasant."

"I agree—but duty first."

Not quite so spoiled after all, she thought as she followed him obediently out of the office.

The shopping trip didn't start off well. Leo stepped aside to make a call and one of the females working at the first shop made a derogatory comment directed at Lily. Unfortunately, he returned in time to hear the end of the assistant's insult and roared with anger. She only barely managed to calm him down and get him out of the shop without violence.

The owner of the next shop was far more accommodating and while his compliments might not have been sincere, they were fulsome enough to satisfy Leo. As a result, she ended up with far more clothes than she thought necessary. When she refused to visit any more shops, he took her to lunch instead. The tiny restaurant had only a few secluded tables overlooking one of the wooded areas of the city. The food was delicious and the service discreet, and although she suspected it was outrageously expensive, she thoroughly enjoyed herself. Maybe having an obscene amount of money wasn't all bad.

After lunch, Leo regretfully informed her that he needed to follow up on some information. He sent for Mata to join her, along with two guards, but she still felt a pang of regret as he strode away.

"Where would you like to go now, Mistress?" Mata asked cheerfully. "More shopping?"

"I certainly don't think I need any more clothes. Unless... is there a lingerie shop?"

Mata ducked her head, obviously embarrassed, but she held a whispered conversation with one of the guards, her tail flicking anxiously, before returning with a suggestion.

The suggested shop was perfect, full of exquisite little scraps of satin and lace that were completely impractical and extraordinarily beautiful. She assembled quite a collection before her conscience intervened and reminded her that she was spending Leo's money.

Leaving the expensive shopping area behind, they ventured into the more cosmopolitan area of the city. While the shops had been almost exclusively populated by Tajiri, the rest of the city was much more diverse, with an astonishing mixture of aliens. Mata showed her some of the places she had discovered the previous night—ranging from a park with a small carousel to a stall selling something unrecognizable but delicious on a long stick.

Leo was waiting for them when they returned, his hands on his hips and his tail lashing. "I did not expect you to be gone so long."

Mata ducked her head, but Lily gave her a reassuring smile and shooed her away before turning to confront Leo. "I wasn't aware that I had a time limit."

"Of course you didn't."

"And I'm sure your guards kept you informed as to our whereabouts." It was purely a guess on her part, but she wasn't surprised when he nodded.

"Well, yes."

"Then what is your problem?" she snapped.

"I - I would have liked to be the one to show you Kalima."

Her heart melted. "It's a big city. I'm sure there are lots of other places you can show me. But I did get this for you."

She handed him the small wrapped package. He looked so astonished that her chest ached, but then he opened the package and pulled out the small toy.

"A paka? Why did you get me this?"

The paka simply looked like a cat to her, but Mata had explained that it was a distant relative of the Tajiri, rather like monkeys and humans.

"Do you remember when we met?"

"I will never forget." His gaze sharpened. "You called me kitty."

"Exactly. And this is a kitty."

She burst into laughter at the look on his face, and took off at a run as he roared. He chased her throughout the apartment, even though she knew he could have caught her at any moment. She accidentally ended up in the kitchen at one point, and stumbled to a halt when everyone looked at her with wide eyes. But then Leo appeared behind her and roared again. She squeaked and started running, and she heard their laughter trailing after her.

He finally caught up with her in the bedroom, tackling her with one flying leap and throwing her onto the mattress.

"Why aren't I surprised that we ended up here?" She laughed up at him, still breathless from the chase.

"Because it's the perfect place to punish a naughty little female who ran from me?"

With one of his lightning-fast moves, he sat up and pulled her over his lap. His tail wrapped around her legs to hold her in place, and then his big hand came down on her ass with a resounding smack. Despite the noise, it left only a slight sting, but that sting went straight to her clit, excitement streaking through her body. He rubbed his hand over the heated spot, squeezing her cheek.

"I think you like that," he purred.

Too embarrassed to admit it out loud, she wiggled her butt against his hand instead, silently asking for more.

CHAPTER TWENTY

Leotra wanted to roar with satisfaction at his female's response, but he didn't want to frighten her. He smacked her delicious ass again, a little harder this time, and the scent of her arousal perfumed the air. The thin cloth of her pants wasn't much of a barrier, but he didn't want anything between them. He yanked them down impatiently, distantly aware of a ripping noise.

"The way you keep tearing my clothes, I can see more shopping in my future," Lily said breathlessly, but he was more focused on the luscious white globes now exposed to his avid gaze.

White except for the slight trace of pink left by his hand. He loved the sight of his marks on her skin, the sign of his claim. He stroked the spot, then slid his hand up to the base of her spine, so bare and vulnerable without a tail.

Apparently tired of his slow exploration, she wiggled her ass again, and he laughed.

"Such an impatient female."

But what his female wanted, she would get. He started

spanking her again, still lightly but hard enough to give a rosy glow to those pale cheeks before he was finished. His cock felt like a blazing metal bar between his legs, aching from the way she had squirmed against him. He slid his hand between her legs, already knowing that he would find her wet. He loved the fact that she was always so ready for him. His fingers brushed lightly across her clit, and she gasped.

"Leo, please."

"Yes, love?"

"I want you. Inside me."

His cock jerked so hard he almost threw her off his lap. He had been doing his best to be patient, to wait for her to be ready.

"Are you sure?" he made himself ask.

She turned her head and glared up at him. "Of course I'm sure. Why would I—"

With a wordless growl, he lifted her off his lap, tossed her face down on the bed, lifted her hips, and sank his cock inside her with one long thrust. She cried out, her channel milking him in exquisite little pulses that threatened to bring on his own climax. But he had waited too long for this. He clenched his jaw and forced himself to remain in place until her tremors finally died away. Her body sagged against the bed, but her sweet little cunt still fisted him in a tight grip.

"One," he said, and she gave a breathless laugh.

"I don't think I can come as many times as I did last night."

"Perhaps not, but we're not done yet," he growled.

He dipped down to gather some of the sweet wetness from between her thighs, then circled her delicate pucker. She shivered, but pushed back against his finger.

"Do you want my finger in your hot little ass?"

When she didn't respond immediately, he pulled away and gave her a quick spank.

"Answer me, love."

"Yes, all right? Yes."

"Good girl," he growled, working his way inside the tiny hole.

The increased tightness to her already impossibly tight cunt made his heart race, but he refused to move until... there. She gave a soft sigh, and her ass relaxed the tiniest fraction before she pushed against his hand. He started to rock into her, keeping his pace slow as his finger echoed the movement.

"Someday I'm going to take you here," he growled. "Push my big cock into this tight little ass until I'm balls deep."

A fresh rush of moisture inside her cunt eased his way, and he sped up, just a little.

"You like that idea, don't you, love?"

When she didn't answer, he gave her ass a warning tap.

"Yes, oh, God, yes."

His hips jerked forward automatically, and they both groaned. His pace increased as his patience began to evaporate. He reached beneath her, holding her in place for his strokes but also so he could press against her clit with each thrust. Lightning streaked down his spine as her body began to convulse around him, and then he was coming in long heated waves as his barbs locked them together.

He carefully pulled his finger free, then collapsed down over her, careful to keep his full weight from crushing her, drained and unbelievably happy. She turned her head and smiled at him.

"I should buy you more pakas."

"You may buy me as many as you wish, although I need no additional incentive to want you."

"But you like chasing me."

"True. I would say that it's instinct, but I've never had the desire before, even when the female was in heat."

Her blunt little teeth closed on her lip. "You mentioned that before. What does it mean?"

"When a Tajiri female is in heat, she is... wetter, more responsive. But you are like that all the time."

"You do seem to have that effect on me," she agreed, but she was still frowning. "Is that the only time they are interested in sex?"

"Of course not. But if they are not in heat, it sometimes requires artificial assistance. Why do you want to know?"

"This. What we have between us. Is it just because I don't need, um, artificial aid?"

"No." His barbs had softened enough that he could pull free, so he sat up and pulled her into his arms.

"I find you infinitely desirable, and I love the fact that your body reveals your desire for me as well. But if we required such aid, I would simply purchase it by the barrel and place it in every room in our house. And every vehicle," he added thoughtfully.

Her cheeks were flushed pink and her eyes oddly bright as she leaned towards him.

"Thank you, Leo," she said quietly.

She kissed him, and even though he would have sworn he was completely drained, his shaft began to harden. But before he could suggest further exploration of her responsiveness, his data pad pinged. He looked over at it, then sighed.

"As much as I would prefer to remain here with you, it is time to prepare for the party."

Her sigh echoed his, but she smiled at him.

"At least we're going together." She wrinkled her nose. "I'd better go take a shower before I get dressed. I smell like sex."

"You smell delightful, but it would be best. Otherwise, all of the males at the party will be following you around like stray pakas."

"You're the only kitty I want," she whispered, then slipped out of his arms.

He smiled after her, but by the time she was dressed, his smile had disappeared beneath the dread of the upcoming evening. He was actually considering canceling when she came to join him. Lust and pride roared through him in equal measure.

Her dress was a pale gold silk that fastened high on her shoulders before dipping down into a deep cowl neckline that revealed the upper swell of her luscious breasts. When she turned in front of him, he saw that the rear neckline dipped even lower, exposing her entire back. On a Tajiri female, the opening would allow for her tail. On Lily, it showed the provocatively smooth, bare flesh above the swell of her buttocks. The dress had no ornamentation, and it needed none. The silky fabric draped across her magnificent figure was ornament enough... except for one thing.

His hands actually threatened to shake as he pulled out his purchase.

"You would honor me by wearing this."

Her eyes widened. "It's beautiful, but I'm not sure I feel comfortable wearing such an expensive necklace."

"It is not just a necklace. It is a mating collar."

"A collar?" Her eyes flew to his face. "I'm not sure I like the implication."

"It is a tradition, or perhaps more accurately, it is a replacement for the original tradition."

"What do you mean?"

"In the past, a Tajiri male would mark his mate by biting her. Here." He ran a finger along the tempting curve of her neck, and she shivered. "Eventually, that became regarded as uncivilized. The mating collar replaced it. Do you not have a symbol to indicate that a couple is joined?"

"We exchange rings," she admitted, still staring at the collar. "And you think this is necessary?"

Oh, yes. He wanted to claim her as his in every way possible. His fangs would have been at her neck in an instant if he thought she would allow it. *Patience*, he reminded himself.

"You agreed to act as my mate," he told her.

"I guess I did. All right, I'll wear it."

She reached for it, but he gently pushed her fingers aside and moved behind her. As the lock clicked into place, satisfaction roared through him so quickly that he had a hard time restraining himself from giving voice to it. *Mine!*

She walked over to the mirror to study it, her fingers lifting to trace the delicate gold band inlaid with gems the exact blue of her eyes.

"Do you like it?" he asked as he came up behind her.

"How could I not? It's beautiful." Their eyes met in the mirror and he could see a question there, but before she spoke, Nargan knocked on the door.

"We are ready to depart, Master Leotra."

Only years of training kept him from snapping at the male. Instead, he picked up her matching cloak and wrapped it around her shoulders as he escorted her down to their vehicle. As he had done with their transport that morning, he had ordered that the windows be tinted so that she would not be afraid. She didn't flinch as they left the garage and flew out into the city.

It was a silent trip. There was so much that he wanted to say to her, but this was not the time or the place. Instead, he leaned back against the seat and watched her, satisfaction filling him every time she turned her head and her collar caught the light. She lifted her hand to it several times, an oddly thoughtful look on her face, but she didn't speak either.

The vessel settled quietly onto the private landing pad at

the mansion, and he bit back another sigh. Time to find out what his father really wanted.

"Come, love."

He held out his hand, and when she took it, an unexpected burst of confidence struck him. Whatever it was, they would face it together.

CHAPTER TWENTY-ONE

Lily clung to Leo's hand as he helped her out of the car and she got her first look around. She had expected it to be grand. The tower was impressive enough, and he had said they were going to a mansion. She hadn't expected something that looked like a more overwrought version of Versailles.

The building—*buildings*—were huge, the walls encrusted with ornamental stonework between a multitude of windows in every shape and size. It was enormous, elaborate—and just the tiniest bit tacky. At least the gardens surrounding the façade were nice.

"Your grandfather built this?"

"No, he bought it once he made his fortune." Leo winced. "My father has added to it."

As they followed a long torchlit path to the door, she saw the enormous gold statues between the torches. Unlike Leo's sensuous sculptures, these were somehow crude, despite their size and obvious expense.

"Let me guess. He picked out the statues?"

He laughed and dropped her hand to put his arm around

her shoulders instead. "Exactly. And this is just the family entrance."

"Is that why you don't live here?"

He shrugged, but she had the impression he was concealing something. "My father and I get along better when we do not live under the same roof."

"What about your grandfather? Did he live here too?"

A shadow crossed his face. "He did, but then he went to a place in the country."

She wanted to press him for more details, but by that time they had arrived at the door and an elaborately dressed male was coming towards them.

"Finally. Really, Leotra, you are most inconsiderate."

"Hello, Father."

Lily took an immediate dislike to Leo's father. Although she could see a certain resemblance between the two, the older male was far more ostentatious. His mane was curled and teased to an astonishing size, while jewels glittered on his hands and at his throat. He cast her a glance that was at once lecherous and dismissive. No, she didn't like him at all.

"And who is this? This is not the occasion for one of your... playthings."

"I think you are confusing my proclivities with yours," Leo growled. "I do not have playthings."

His father shrugged an impatient shoulder. "You may choose whatever term you like. However, I arranged this dinner in order for you to make the acquaintance of—"

"I don't think you understand. Lily, this is my father, Chinit. Father, this is Lily. My mate."

The warmth and pride in his voice almost brought tears to her eyes, and she pressed closer to his side.

"What? You cannot be serious." The older male actually seemed to stagger, his tail whipping out behind him.

"I'm quite serious." Leo unfastened her cloak, revealing her mating collar.

"No," his father whispered, his eyes fixed on the band of gold.

She'd had mixed feelings about the collar. The obvious symbolism bothered her, but when he had placed it around her neck, it had felt as if he was placing a ring on her finger. In the face of his father's shock, she lifted her chin proudly.

"But she's human," Chinit protested. "Humans are for fucking, not for mating."

Leo growled and seized his father by the neck of his elaborate robe. "I never want to hear you say anything like that again."

"Leo!" She tugged urgently on his arm as his father choked. "He's your father. It's not worth it."

Her words seemed to penetrate, and he finally released his grip. His father straightened his robe, his face furious as he glared at her.

"His name is Leotra va Situni, not Leo."

Really? That was what he wanted to be a dick about? Leo growled again, but she put a restraining hand on his arm as she gave his father a sweet smile.

"And my name is Lily va Situni and I can call him whatever I like. Now, let's go inside, *Leo*."

Leo smiled down at her as he escorted her through the massive doors.

"What?"

"Lily va Situni."

She could feel the heat rising in her cheeks.

"Was it wrong of me to say that?"

"On the contrary. I enjoyed hearing it very much. I can't wait to hear it again when you're naked in my arms."

She didn't need to look down to know her nipples were

pressing against her dress. "Maybe we'd better get out of here first."

"I'm afraid you're right. Come, let me introduce you to a few people."

The party was an odd combination of elegance and depravity. In some rooms people sprawled in drunken abandon, while in others they danced to what sounded like classical music. On one of the terraces a group was playing something that reminded her of cornhole, but beyond them she could also see half-naked people chasing each other through a maze.

"And I thought rock bands threw wild parties," she murmured.

"Does it bother you?" he asked. "We can leave."

"It's fine. As long as no one is being forced to do something they don't want to do, I don't care how people choose to enjoy themselves."

Fortunately, the people he wanted her to meet were in some of the more restrained rooms. All of them were remarkably gracious, even though she could see the surprise on their faces.

"A most charming mate," an older male said, bowing over her hand. "And very fashionable."

"That's not why I chose her," Leo growled and the male ducked his head apologetically.

"No, of course not."

"What was that about?" Lily asked as they walked away.

"The new Emperor's mate is human—" He stopped and looked around. "Damn, the Mafanan ambassador just went into the pet room."

"There are animals here?"

"Not those kinds of pets," he said, and she blushed. "Don't worry, I have no intention of taking you in there. But I would like to talk to him and make sure he understands the importance of trying to find your friends. There won't be anyone in the library. Would you mind waiting there for me?"

"As long as you don't start looking for a pet of your own."

"You're the only female I want, love."

The look in his eyes made her heart pound. She couldn't think of anything to say, but he didn't seem to expect a response. Instead, he led her into a massive library. Two stories of shelves filled three of the walls, while the other consisted of tall windows overlooking the gardens.

"I'll be back as soon as I can," he promised.

She wandered along the bookcases, wishing she could read the Tajiri language. She decided she would ask Leo to teach her, but for now, she found a book filled with pictures of gardens and she carried it over to a window seat. Long curtains framed each of the windows and when she heard someone enter the room, she instinctively drew back behind the curtain.

"You were supposed to distract him," a voice hissed, and she realized with a start that it was Leo's father.

"He wasn't interested." The other voice was low and sultry, female.

"I should have sent someone younger. You're losing your appeal."

"You bastard. You weren't so rude when you were trying to get me in your bed."

"I didn't have to try very hard," Chinit said coldly. "You're a slut, Jinga."

Lily couldn't help a sympathetic wince.

"Maybe so," Jinga hissed. "At least I had enough experience to know that your tiny little cock would never please me."

Chinit snarled and for a moment Lily wondered if she would have to intervene, but then she heard the door slam and realized that the female had left. A moment later, the door opened again, and when she peeped cautiously around the edge of the curtain, the library was empty once more.

She was still thinking about the conversation when Leo reappeared. He looked tired and annoyed, and she put her arms around him.

"No luck?" she asked softly.

"No, I found him. He promised me he would look into it."

"Then what's wrong?"

"We've always had parties here, and the entertainment has always... varied. But this just feels sleazy. My grandfather would never have allowed it to get this far."

"You said he left the mansion? Why?"

"There was an argument," he said shortly, and she decided not to pursue the matter.

"Can we go home now?"

"Home. Yes, I like the sound of that." He ran his finger along her collar as he used his communicator to send for Nargan.

The trip home was as silent as their journey to the mansion, but as soon as they arrived back at the apartment, he carried her up to their bedroom. He stripped off everything except her collar and made love to her with such slow, passionate intensity that silent tears dripped down her cheeks. Her heart ached as he drew her into his arms afterwards, and she suddenly realized how much she wished that they were truly mated.

CHAPTER TWENTY-TWO

"You must be mistaken." Leotra glared at Captain Nargan.
"I am afraid not," the guard said apologetically. "Based on everything that I have been able to discover, the business is being used as a front for a slaving operation."

A sick feeling filled his stomach. If whoever was running the operation had chosen to conceal its activities, that meant that they were not obeying the Imperial laws concerning slavery. Just like the bastards who had stolen Lily in the first place.

"I will not permit it. And as soon as I find out who is behind it, they will be lucky if they ever see daylight again."

"Yes, sir. I will start assembling a squad. I suggest that we wait and move after dark. That way, we may be able to catch some of the buyers as well."

"Make it so."

Nargan departed, leaving Leotra staring down at his desk. How was he going to tell Lily that one of his own companies had been used as a front for slavery?

The thought of the female he had left sleeping in his bed made his chest ache. He didn't like this pretense. It was time to tell her that she was his true mate. That it was not an act on his part. He thought—he hoped—that she was beginning to feel the same way about him.

But he needed to resolve this matter first, and as much as he hated it, that meant he needed to speak to his father again. The registered owner of the company was Bintir, one of his father's long-standing business associates. He owed it to his father to let him know what the treacherous male had been doing.

He reached for the communicator, then hesitated. He suspected that if he tried to convey the information from a distance, his father would simply hang up on him. Perhaps it would be best to confront him directly.

"Good morning." Lily's soft voice interrupted him, and he looked up to see her standing in the doorway of his office. Her eyes were still heavy with sleep, her hair tousled, and she was dressed simply in one of his shirts, her long bare legs peeking out from beneath the hem. His collar was still fastened around her neck. He held out his hand, and she came to him immediately, curling into his lap with a contented sigh.

"I left orders to let you sleep," he murmured against her head.

"I woke up when you weren't there. I missed you."

"I missed you too."

"More work?"

"I'm afraid so. I will need to go and speak to my father today."

She sniffed disdainfully, and he almost laughed. Most females were impressed by his parent, but Lily had seen through him immediately.

"Will you come with me?" he added. "There's someone else I want you to meet."

"If you want me to come."

She didn't sound enthusiastic, but he laughed and hugged her. "I think you will find this visit far more entertaining."

"All right. How soon do we have to leave?" Her fingers brushed lightly across his cock.

"Not that soon."

She laughed as he picked her up and carried her back to bed.

Unfortunately, that laughter had disappeared by the time they pulled up in front of the mansion once more.

"Do I have to meet him again?"

"No, love." He thought for a moment, then led her around the side of the main building and through a door concealed in an ancient brick wall. The garden that awaited them was slightly wild but lush with flowers, full of private nooks and hidden grottos.

"It's a secret garden!" she exclaimed in delight.

"Yes, it was dedicated to my grandmother. No one will disturb you here."

She nodded absently, bending down to sniff at a flowering bloom. *She looks at home here*, he thought, *just as she did in the jungle*. The natural environment suited her better than the more elaborate surroundings that were so much a part of his life.

He kissed her, and left her there, assigning a guard to wait outside the wall. No one ever entered the space without permission.

Lily explored the garden after Leo left, discovering new delights around every corner. As she ducked under a low-hanging vine, she saw an old Tajiri male, digging in the dirt of one of the beds. Since Leo said no one ever came here, she decided he must be a gardener. She was about to retreat and leave him to his work when he looked up at her.

Surprisingly sharp blue eyes studied her face and she half-expected him to demand to know her business. Instead, his gaze slipped down to the collar around her neck and he snorted, then shook his head.

"Newfangled ways. The boy should have mated you properly."

"The boy? Do you mean Leo?"

A bushy eyebrow arched, the expression oddly familiar.

"Are you mated to anyone else?"

She laughed and shook her head. She should have realized that the servants would know everything.

"No, he's more than enough for me."

"Is he?"

"Yes." She had the oddest desire to burst into tears. "He's been very good to me."

Another snort. "I can see that. Got an Emperor's ransom around your neck."

"That's not what I meant. I don't care about the jewelry."

"Then what did you mean?"

He was considerably blunter than any of the other servants she had encountered, but then again, perhaps his age gave him courage—and she had never minded plain speaking.

Somehow, she found herself telling him everything that had happened from the moment she woke up on the slavers' ship. He kept working, shooting her an occasional glance from underneath those bushy brows, but he asked very few questions.

"Good thing you came along," he said finally when she brought him up to date.

"What do you mean?"

"Too many females chasing him. I never trusted one of them."

It was sweet that even the servants were protective about Leo, but she had noticed that they all seemed to care about him. "I'm glad I came along too." *But will it last?* she wondered. He had never said that he wanted her to stay forever, but she had begun to suspect that he was considering it.

"Would you like some help with the weeding?" she asked, changing the subject before she started tearing up again.

"You'll mess up your pretty clothes."

"I know," she laughed. "I told Leo they weren't very practical. I miss my jeans."

"Jeans?" he asked as she knelt down next to him. He handed her a trowel.

As they worked, she told him about her life on Earth. He listened, grunting occasionally, and only rarely asking a blunt question.

They had just reached the end of the bed, when Leo stormed up, his face like a thundercloud.

"He is impossible!" he snarled, then saw her companion and flinched. "Grandfather!"

"Oh, so you still remember who I am?"

"Of course I do. Lily, this is my grandfather, Kubwan."

"He's your grandfather?" She suddenly realized why some of his gestures had seemed so familiar. "I thought he was dead."

"Why did you tell her that? I may be old, but I'm not dead."

Leo scowled. "I never said that."

"I misunderstood," she said quickly. "He said that he hadn't seen you in a long time and that he missed you. I just assumed that you were gone."

"You didn't have to miss me," the older male said gruffly. "You knew where I was."

"Father said you didn't want to see me."

"And you believed him? I told him I didn't want to see him, but it never extended to you."

"I hoped you would forgive me. I heard you were back and I was bringing Lily to see you. But I had to deal with Father first."

Leo sighed, looking tired and frustrated, and she climbed to her feet and went to his side. He put his arm around her, and she felt some of the tension leave his body.

"Every time I think he can't get any worse, he manages to do just that," he muttered.

"What is it now?"

Leo shot her guilty look, and her heart started to pound.

"I am truly sorry, love, but it appears that one of our companies is being used as a front for a slave ring. It's owned by one of his cronies, and he refuses to believe what I told him."

"A slave ring?" Her heart raced. "You don't think they might have my friends, do you?"

"I don't know, but I intend to find out. We are arranging a raid on the place tonight." He tugged her tighter against him as he looked over at his grandfather. "You don't seem very surprised."

"I still have connections in the city. I heard rumors that he was pursuing some undesirable income streams." For the first time, the old man looked his age. "How did he turn out so poorly?"

"It wasn't him," Leo protested. "Bintir is responsible."

His grandfather shot him a look, but didn't comment. Instead, he extended a hand to Leo and, when Leo stepped forward and took it, pulled him into a bone crushing hug.

"You are always welcome in my house, boy," he muttered. "I should have ignored my foolish pride and told you directly."

"You always were a stubborn old man."

"And you were always an impudent youngster."

The two of them grinned at each other, and Lily rolled her eyes.

"Did your father tell you anything else?" Kubwan asked.

"What do you mean?"

His grandfather sighed. "I must admit I'm not really surprised. Give me a minute to clean up and then the three of us will talk to him."

"Is that necessary?"

"Oh, yes. Wait here." Then he looked at Lily. "Or maybe you had better get her cleaned up as well."

"I would like to at least wash my hands," she agreed. "Although I'm not sure that the outfit is salvageable."

"It doesn't matter," Leo assured her. "You are still beautiful."

Kubwan grunted and led them out of the walled garden and into a part of the mansion she hadn't seen the previous night. The rooms were still oversized, but it had a much cozier feel.

"These are my private quarters. At least Chinit hasn't tried to confiscate them yet."

"Can he do that?" she asked.

The old man grinned. "He could try, but he wouldn't get very far. I'll be right back."

While he was gone, Lily washed her hands but decided her pants were past saving. Leo stared off into space as she brushed them down the best she could.

"Hey. What are you thinking?"

"That I don't like not knowing what's going on."

"I have a feeling you're about to find out."

He gave her a reluctant smile. "I'm afraid so."

Kubwan reappeared a few minutes later, unexpectedly imposing in a formal robe.

"Follow me," he ordered.

They dutifully obeyed as he shepherded them back into the main part of the mansion and then into a study. Unlike Leo's office, the room did not seem to be designed for work. There were no papers on the enormous desk and Chinit was lounging in front of the fire with a female kneeling at his feet.

Kubwan snorted. "Hard at work as usual, I see."

"Father. What are you doing here?" His dislike was obvious, and it didn't lessen as he looked at Leo. "And why are you back? I told you that I had no further interest in your wild speculations."

"It's not speculation—" Leo began, but his grandfather shook his head.

"We'll come back to that. I believe there is something your father forgot to tell you, isn't that right, Chinit?"

"I have no idea what you're talking about," Chinit said arrogantly, but Lily thought he looked frightened.

"You mean you've forgotten the clause in our agreement that gives Leotra full control of his inheritance once he is mated?"

The girl at his feet gasped, and Chinit scowled at her. "Leave us. And keep your mouth shut." As she scurried out of the room, he turned back to them, his arrogance firmly in place.

"What difference does it make? Leotra has no interest in the company."

"That's a lie and you know it. You've done your best to keep me out of it, but it wasn't because I wasn't interested," Leo growled at his father and turned to his grandfather. "What do you mean full control of my inheritance?"

"What I mean is that you now have a controlling interest in the company."

"No wonder you were so upset when I told you that Lily and I were mated," Leo said.

"A human mate doesn't count."

"Of course she does," Kubwan snapped.

"That's why you sent Jinga to distract him," Lily said, putting the pieces together. "You didn't want him mating anyone, and you knew he'd never choose her."

Three sets of eyes fastened on her face. Kubwan looked disgusted, Leo appalled, and Chinit furious.

"You don't know what you're talking about," he snarled.

"Yes, I do. I was in the library last night. I'm sorry," she added, turning to Leo. "They never mentioned your name, and I didn't realize until now who they were discussing."

"It's not your fault." Leo turned to his father. "I am calling a board meeting tomorrow morning to inform them of the change in leadership. You are not welcome."

"You can't just shut me out!"

"Of course he can," Kubwan cackled. "I think I'll enjoy attending that meeting."

"I look forward to seeing you there," Leo said. "And perhaps, we can talk afterwards?"

"Aye. Now take your pretty mate home. I have more things to say to Chinit."

Leo didn't hesitate. He put his arm around her shoulders and urged her out of the room.

CHAPTER TWENTY-THREE

Leotra's head still reeled as he escorted Lily back to their vehicle. She seemed to understand, not asking him any questions as they returned home. They made it as far as his rooftop sitting area before she gave him a sympathetic smile.

"Do you want to talk about it?"

"I don't know what to say," he admitted.

She came and curled up next to him. "You really didn't know about the mating clause?"

"No, but now that I do, some things make a lot more sense." *Like the number of unsuitable females who chased after me.* Not that he was about to discuss that with Lily.

"I can't believe he sent someone to seduce you," she muttered, obviously following the same train of thought.

"Someone he knew would never arouse more than a passing interest."

Her brows drew together. "But you thought I was like her."

"No, I didn't. But despite what my instincts were telling me, I couldn't help but be suspicious."

"What were your instincts telling you?"

"That you were perfect for me."

The soft pink washed over her cheeks, but somewhat to his surprise, she changed the subject.

"What happened between you and your grandfather?"

"We had a huge fight—over my father, of all things. Grandfather told me that he was sleeping with the female I was seeing, but I didn't believe him. Of course, it turned out that he was right."

"But you believed your father when he told you your grandfather didn't want to see you?"

He shrugged uncomfortably. "I couldn't blame him for being angry. But I think that it was more than that. I was ashamed."

"Why were you ashamed?"

"I told you he built an entire empire by the time he was my age. And all I was doing was chasing worthless females and wasting time."

"You said you didn't have any authority in the company."

"I know, but I think I should have done more. Or maybe I should have just left and started my own company."

"It's never too late," she said softly.

"You really mean that, don't you? You would come with me and leave all of this behind?"

"Of course I would." She looked down at her hands. "I've moved on so many times. I always thought I was just trying to find the right place. But now I realize the place doesn't matter at all." Her eyes lifted to his. "Only the person you're with matters. And as long as we're together, I don't care where we are or what we're doing."

An enormous weight lifted off his shoulders. "I love you, Lily. I should have told you a long time ago."

Her eyes sparkled with tears, but she smiled at him. "I love you too."

Thank the gods.

He ran his finger along her mating collar. "And you should know that this was never a fake mating for me. I meant what I said the very first time. You're mine."

"I-I think I felt the same way, but I was too scared to admit it. To trust you."

"I didn't exactly make it easy," he admitted.

"No, but now I understand why you were so suspicious." She buried her fingers in his mane, tugging his head down so that she could kiss him.

It was a sweet kiss, but he could feel the urgency beginning to build in his body. When he finally raised his head, she gave him a speculative look.

"I discovered this morning that I can't take off the mating collar."

"No. It's keyed to my thumbprint."

"I suspected something like that. Please take it off."

Panic raced through his system. "No! You said you loved me. You said you were my mate."

"I do love you, and I do want to be your mate," she said patiently. "That's why I want you to take off the collar."

"I don't understand."

"I want to do this the old-fashioned way. I want you to use your mouth on me."

Lily felt Leo's muscles freeze, and then he was fumbling impatiently at her neck. It took him three times before he managed to release the catch, and then he flung the expensive necklace aside, burying his face in her neck. For a second, she thought he meant to bite her immediately, but he only licked the spot, sending pleasurable shivers down her spine.

"We are going to do this properly," he mumbled, rising up with her in his arms and striding off to the bedroom.

He stripped off her clothes eagerly, then laid her down on the bed. For a long moment, he did nothing but look at her, which shouldn't have been erotic, but she could feel her nipples harden and her pussy dampen just from the intensity in her gaze.

"You are so beautiful."

"You're pretty beautiful yourself. But you would be more so with fewer clothes."

He laughed and tugged off his clothing before he joined her on the bed.

"You know, traditionally, I would mount you from behind."

Mmm. She had no objection—she loved the feel of his big body pressing against her.

"But I don't want to this time. I want to see you come. I want to know that you see me."

"Okay," she whispered, and he smiled.

"But first, I'm going to worship you."

And he did. He feasted on her breasts until her nipples throbbed in tune with her heartbeat. He spent just as long on her pussy, but he never pushed her over into a climax, easing off each time she got close.

"I think you're ready," he said at last.

Her entire body was alive with sensation, even the brush of air against her skin an exquisite torture.

"I've been ready," she gasped.

"Slowly," he said, but she thought he was talking to himself rather than to her as she finally felt his cock at the entrance to her pussy.

He entered her with agonizing slowness, his thick cock easing into the slick, swollen passage an inch at a time until he filled her completely. His barbs stirred, stroking the sensitive areas inside her channel and she could feel her climax hovering just out of reach.

Blue eyes blazed down at her. "I love you, Lily."

"I love you too."

She tipped her head to one side, baring her neck in silent invitation, and he groaned. His mouth closed down over the tender flesh, sucking it into his mouth. She could feel the prick of his fangs, but she wasn't afraid.

"Claim me," she whispered.

His mouth clamped down, his fangs sinking into her flesh. She had expected it to hurt, but instead it sent her flying into an overwhelming climax. She was lost in an explosion of pleasure so intense that the world sheeted white and she was only vaguely aware of his answering growl, of his cock swelling inside her as his barbs locked them together.

He was still shuddering against her when her senses returned, and she combed her fingers through his mane until his body finally relaxed. He lifted his head and smiled down at her.

"One."

Her eyes widened as she realized that his cock was still rigid inside her. He flexed his hips, not enough to disturb the barbs, but enough to make her channel flutter around him. Her neck throbbed in a pleasurable, erotic way.

"But we're still locked together," she protested weakly.

"Don't worry, love. I won't let that stop me."

And he didn't.

CHAPTER TWENTY-FOUR

Leotra stared around at the empty warehouse in dismay and growing anger. The building was empty. Only a few portable cages remained behind.

"They were warned."

"Yes, sir." Nargan shook his head. "I should have set a better watch, but I didn't want to tip them off."

"It's not your fault." He had a horrible suspicion that he knew exactly who was to blame. His bastard father. "But search the place. See if you can find any indication of who was here or where they might have gone."

He didn't really expect the guards to turn up anything, but a short time later Nargan returned with a Ceekat male in tow. The stench of alcohol emanating from his body was so strong that Leotra almost gagged.

"Found him passed out in the toilet. Says his name is Tothra. He claims he doesn't know what happened."

The male blinked at him, his eyes bleary. "I just came to make a purchase."

"You have enough money to buy a slave?" Leotra asked doubtfully, surveying the male's ragged clothing.

"Not 'xactly. I found an unclaimed female so I traded her in." Tothra surveyed the empty space sadly. "But I never got my end of the deal. Probably why they kept giving me liquor."

"A female?" he growled, trying not to lose his temper.

"Yeah. They like those. But she was too small. And soft." Tothra shuddered. "I like 'em big and hard. Get the old juices flowing, you know what I mean?"

Tothra tried to nudge him, but Leotra pulled away in disgust.

"What was the female like?"

"I told you. Small. Soft. Yellow hair."

"Was she human?" he demanded.

"Maybe? Sounds kind of familiar. One of your males bought her."

"One of my males?"

"Yeah. A buk-, a bukh—you know, one of them." Tothra pointed at the guards.

"None of my males would do such a thing," Nargan snapped.

"Looked like one of you. Say, you don't have anything to drink, do you?"

"No," he said shortly. "Take him away, Nargan. See if we can get more out of him once he's sobered up."

"Yes, sir."

"Leave a few men here to keep searching, but I need to return to the apartment. And to contact my grandfather."

And somehow he needed to find a way to tell his mate that he might have missed the chance to rescue one of her friends.

. . .

LILY paced back and forth anxiously. Leo and the guards had left to raid the slave ring, and he had refused to let her accompany them.

"It's too dangerous. You will be safe here. The doors are locked, and no one can enter."

"That's not what I'm worried about. What if you find Kate or Mary? Or another human? I should be there to let them know that they're safe now."

"I promise you that I will bring any humans I find directly to you."

"I suppose. But please be gentle. I can't stand to think what might have happened to them."

"As gentle as a paka," he promised with a teasing smile.

"Good kitty."

He gave a mock growl, grabbed her ass, and hauled her against him.

"We'll come back to this later," he promised.

Then he kissed her and was gone.

Mata kept her company at first, but the girl was equally worried about Janob and her nervous speculations only added to Lily's anxiety. In the end, Lily did her best to give her a reassuring smile and sent her off to assist the chef in making treats for the return of the males.

She knew that Leo was strong and fast, and she knew that the guards were well-trained, but as the time ticked past, more and more horrible scenarios tried to creep into her mind. It seemed like he had been gone forever, leaving her nothing to do except wait and pace—which was why she had ended up in the entry corridor. There was plenty of room to move, and at least she would be the first to know when Leo returned.

She finally decided to go check on Mata again, but as she reached the stairs, she heard the outer doors open. She spun around eagerly, a welcoming smile on her lips, but only a single person stepped through the doors—a tall Tajiri male wearing a cloak. Her heart skipped a beat. Had something happened to Leo?

Then the male threw back the hood of his cloak. *Chinit.*

Leo's father looked terrible, his elegantly styled mane in a wild tangle around his shoulders, and his face worn and angry.

"What are you doing here?"

"I'm going to put an end to this ridiculous nonsense," he snarled. "The Situni corporation is mine."

"Not any longer. You need to leave before—"

"Before your precious *Leo* returns?" He laughed, the sound high-pitched and unstable. "He's too busy chasing his tail at an empty warehouse."

"How do you know it's empty?"

She took a careful step backwards as she spoke, frantically trying to think of a plan. Her heel bumped against the bottom step.

"How do you think? It was my idea. Of course, it was kind of Leotra to warn me in time to get the slaves out of there. I would have hated to lose all my inventory."

"*Your* idea?" She gave him a horrified stare. "How could you? They aren't inventory. They're people!"

"Not to me," he said callously.

"Leave our home. Now," she ordered.

"Your home? Don't make me laugh. This is part of the Situni Tower. That means it belongs to me."

She glared at him. "Not based on what I heard this afternoon. It doesn't sound like anything belongs to you anymore."

He snarled again. "Don't you play games with me, bitch. I know that this mating is just a sham."

"No, it's not."

"Of course it is. I told you before. Humans are for fucking, not for mating."

She lifted her chin defiantly, even as he prowled closer. "Leo doesn't seem to agree with you."

"Oh, he agrees with me. He just needed someone gullible enough to go along with it so that he could claim his inheritance."

For the briefest moment, the old doubts washed over her. Was it possible that Leo had known about the clause and had just been using her all along? Chinit must have seen the hesitation on her face because he smiled triumphantly.

"I don't believe you," she said, with all the conviction she could muster. "He's handsome, wealthy, and charming. He could have anyone he wanted."

"Yes, but if he chose a Tajiri female, he would be mated for life." Chinit sneered at her. "You're disposable. As soon as he gets tired of fucking you, he'll take off that collar and be free to do whatever he wants."

The momentary flicker of doubt disappeared, replaced by a deep certainty. She knew Leo. She trusted him. She gave Chinit a sweet smile and pushed her gown away from her neck.

"This isn't disposable. A mating mark is for life."

His eyes blazed with fury, and he raised a hand, claws fully extended.

"We'll see about that. I'll cut it out of your flesh before I let him choose a human over me."

Her instincts screamed at her to run, but she knew he could catch her. Instead, she reached behind her, finding the metal sculpture of the lovers.

Chinit took a step closer, and she ducked, twisting as she did to grab the statue with both hands. She whirled back around and swung it against his extended arm as if she was swinging a baseball bat. The bone broke with a sickening crack, and he howled, but the rage on his face only intensified. He seized the statue with his intact arm. She tried to hang onto it, but he was far stronger and it slipped out of her grasp.

"I'm going to enjoy making you pay for that," he snarled. His hand clenched painfully around her wrist as he started to drag her back down the corridor.

L*EOTRA RACED THROUGH THE ENTRANCE DOORS JUST IN* time to see his father grab hold of Lily. His roar filled the enclosed space as he charged at them, prying Chinit's hand away from her and throwing him against the wall.

"You dare. You dare to lay a hand on my female. It will be the last thing you ever do."

Terror filled Chinit's face as Leo advanced towards him. He relished the sight, fury racing through his blood, but then Lily's soft hand touched his arm.

"You can't kill him, Leo."

"He touched you," he growled.

"Yes, but he's your father."

"Not any longer. He is a despicable male." His eyes flicked to her face, hating to break the news to her. "I'm sorry, love. The warehouse was empty. The bastard warned them."

"I know," she said quietly. "He told me."

Chinit began to laugh, despite the blood running down his face. "It certainly took you long enough to work that out. And you can spare me your righteous indignation. You have your own human slave."

"She is not my slave. She is my mate." *My everything.*

"How touching," Chinit sneered. "But I am still a member of House Situni."

"No, you're not. I spoke to Grandfather on the way back here. As of now, your access to any Situni assets has been terminated. You have no business, no property, and no funds."

He stepped back and gestured to Captain Nargan, waiting silently behind them with his squad. "Take him away."

Chinit howled in rage but he was no match for two of the big Bukharans.

"I think I broke his arm," Lily murmured as Chinit wailed.

"Good. My fierce mate." He pulled her against him and buried his face in her red curls. "Can you ever forgive me?"

"Why do I need to forgive you?"

"I was the one who warned him. It's my fault that the slaves are gone."

"You didn't know. I didn't like him, but I had no idea that he would stoop that low. What's going to happen to him?"

"He will face the Imperial Court. A nice little stint on a prison planet might help him see the error of his ways."

"And your grandfather really cut him off?"

"He did. That's how I knew he was here. We saw that he had accessed the outer doors when we were terminating his account." He shuddered at the memory of the terror that had raced through him when he realized Chinit had gone after Lily. "Yet another reason I am at fault. I locked the doors but it never occurred to me that as a family member, he would still have access."

"It's all right. Everything worked out in the end."

Her hands stroked his arm soothingly, even though she had been the one in danger as a result of his actions.

"I don't deserve you."

"Probably not." She grinned up at him. "But I'm not sure I deserve you either. We'll just have to work on that. I have a few suggestions."

"Oh?"

"I think we should start with a nice peaceful swim. And then it's your turn to lie back while I have my way with you."

His guilt disappeared in a wave of desire as he lifted her

into his arms and headed for the roof. It was a sacrifice he was prepared to make.

A very long time later, Leotra stared up at the night sky. The lights of the city prevented him from seeing the stars, but he knew that they were there. Millions of stars and millions of planets, but somehow, miraculously, Lily had found her way to him.

She slept peacefully in his arms, worn out by her efforts in the pool. *Her very remarkable efforts*, he thought with an appreciative flex of his cock at the memory. He realized he had forgotten to tell her about the possibility that one of her friends might have been in the warehouse, but Nargan already had a search in progress. There would be time to tell her tomorrow. They had all the time in the world.

EPILOGUE

Nine months later...

Lily hid in the undergrowth beneath one of the huge trees in the Sayari jungle, her heart racing. She had heard Leo pass by only a few minutes earlier, and she wasn't sure if she had managed to fool him this time. Cautiously lowering a leaf, she tried to peer out of her hiding place without giving herself away. The clearing looked empty, and she debated making a run for it. But just as she decided to take the chance, a massive body tackled her, rolling over so that he hit the ground first and cradled her fall.

"Gotcha," he growled.

"I'm never going to be able to escape you, am I?" She mock pouted.

"Never." His eyes went to the mating mark on her neck with immense satisfaction. "You are mine."

"But you still like to chase me."

"And you still like to be chased."

He was right. She loved the rush of adrenaline, even though she knew he would never harm her. And when he caught her? Her pussy was already wet with anticipation.

"Although I don't understand why you insist on wearing these," he grumbled, tracing his finger down her bra strap, his claws already threatening to emerge. "You know I'm only going to rip them off of you."

"Because they're pretty. And because you enjoy ripping them off of me." So much so that she suspected she had become the lingerie shop's biggest customer.

Her nipple peeked through the appliquéd flowers that formed the minimal cups, and she shivered as his claw popped out and teased the rosy peak.

"They are pretty," he agreed. He plucked at the strap of the matching thong, working it back and forth and teasing her sensitive bottom hole. "But you are far more beautiful."

As he started to tug her towards him to feast on her nipples, she heard the communicator hidden in his loincloth make a soft ping.

"Ignore it," she urged him. "We're on holiday."

He had spent the last nine months trying to repair all of the damage his father had done to the company. She could see the strain it had put on him, and she had finally conspired with his grandfather to practically kidnap him and take him back to Sayari for a well-deserved rest.

The break from routine had appealed to her as well. In an effort to assist him, she had started managing the many social events that were an integral part of the way the Tajiri did business. Somewhat to her surprise, she found that not only was she good at it but that she rather enjoyed it, but she wanted this time alone with him even more.

"Your grandfather will handle it," she reminded him now.

The older man had promised to take care of everything while they were on Sayari.

"I have to check. What if something has happened to him?"

The thought made her heart skip a beat. She had grown as fond of Leo's grandfather as if he was her own grandfather.

"You're right."

He pulled out the communicator and checked it quickly. His body tensed.

"What is it? Please tell me he's okay."

"It's not Grandfather. It's a message from Captain Nargan."

The rush of relief made her even more angry that he'd disturbed them. "Really? What couldn't wait?"

"He received word from Mafana. Someone is trying to find you. The message says her name is Kate."

"Kate?" The jungle whirled around her. They had spent so long looking for her friends—and every lead had seemed to reach a dead-end. She had almost given up hope, even though Leo insisted on continuing the search.

"Yes."

"But the Mafanan ambassador said that no humans had been abandoned there."

"I don't understand it either," he admitted. "But it's the first real lead we've had since we started searching."

"Is she all right? Where is she? Can we go there?"

She scrambled her feet, wincing apologetically when her knee rammed into his cock.

"You know, another five minutes wouldn't make any difference," he said, stroking his abused cock with a pitiful look.

"You would never be satisfied with five minutes," she told him. "And there is a bed on the ship. I can spend the whole journey soothing your wounded... pride."

"Now that sounds like a reason to hurry," he agreed,

leaping to his feet and throwing her over his shoulder as she squealed with laughter, her heart filled with hope.

Please let it be Kate, please let it be Kate, she prayed as they raced back to the lodge.

"You tricked me," Leo growled in her ear as the boat they had rented glided across the green Mafanan ocean.

"What do you mean?"

"You didn't spend the entire trip soothing my... pride."

She giggled. "I didn't mean to fall asleep. It was your fault. You made me come so many times I couldn't keep my eyes open."

"I'll just have to keep working on your stamina."

An anticipatory shiver rolled across her body as she leaned back into his arms. "I can hardly wait."

His arms tightened around her as they watched the waves skim by. Sea birds circled far overhead, and the warm ocean air suddenly reminded her of Cosmo Beach.

"This is so beautiful. I had forgotten how much I love the ocean."

"There is an ocean on Yangu as well," Leo reminded her. "I believe we even own a house there. Would you like to visit it when we return?"

"I'd love to."

"No one has been there for a long time, so I'm not sure what kind of shape it's in," he warned. "And I don't think it's very big."

"That sounds even better."

"I told you that we didn't have to live in the mansion." They had moved in after his father's unceremonious departure.

"I know, but I didn't want to leave your grandfather there

alone. I'm getting used to it—but it would be nice to have some place smaller just for us."

"I'll look into it as soon as we return," he promised, then pointed to the front of the boat. "I think that's our destination."

A tropical island rose out of the water ahead of them, lush with vegetation. A pretty village of square white buildings followed the curve of a bay, but they headed for the rocky point at one end. A sprawling white castle climbed up the rocks, festooned with flowering vines.

As they pulled up to the dock, a tall Mafanan male came to join them. In one of the few intervals when they weren't making love and she wasn't asleep, Leo had briefed her on the Mafanans. She knew that what looked like his legs were actually tentacles that would unfurl when he entered the water, but she wouldn't have guessed by looking at him. He was very good-looking in an austere sort of way, with deep teal-colored skin and large golden eyes.

"I am Prince A'tai of House Maulimu. You are Lily?"

"Yes, and this is my mate, Leotra va Situni. Where is Kate?" she asked eagerly.

"She is on the terrace. She is still weak, and I would not permit her to come down and meet you."

Her heart started to race. "Weak? What's wrong with her?"

"She is still recovering from the birth."

"The birth?" Kate had a baby? The same woman who had pulled a face anytime Mary talked about her kindergarten class? Had this strange male forced her to give birth?

But when they reached the terrace and she saw Kate cradling her child, her face warm with happiness, her doubts disappeared. There was no doubt that she loved her daughter. A'tai checked to make sure that Kate didn't need anything, then he, Leo, and Nargan left them alone to talk.

"This is Marli," Kate said proudly. "I named her after you and Mary."

Unexpected tears sprang to Lily's eyes as she admired the baby. Her skin was a soft, pearly white and she had a tiny tuft of brown hair, but when her eyes blinked open, they were as large and golden as her father's.

"She's beautiful."

"Yes, she is," Kate said complacently. "Now sit down and tell me everything that's happened to you. I can't believe we've been so close all this time and didn't know it."

"The Mafanan ambassador told Leo there weren't any humans here."

"We don't spend a lot of time in the capital, but it's hard to believe he hadn't heard about me. Unless my evil mother-in-law told him to keep silent."

"You have an evil mother-in-law?"

A guilty expression crossed Kate's face. "I shouldn't say that. She can be... difficult, but she usually has good intentions. She might have told him to say that because she thought she was protecting me. Or A'tai. And I have to admit that she's a wonderful grandmother."

Kate told her more about how she'd met A'tai and her encounters with his mother, and then Lily filled her in on her own experiences.

"And you couldn't find out anything else about Mary?"

Lily shook her head. "We're not even one hundred percent positive it was her. The witness said that was her name, but he wasn't very reliable. He did seem pretty sure that a Bukharan bought her, but the trail went cold after that."

Both women looked over at the Bukharan captain, and Lily sighed. "I know that Nargan is a very honorable male. My friend Mata is also mated to a Bukharan, and she's very happy. But they're so big and Mary is so small."

"I have found that a large size is very pleasurable," Kate said calmly, and Lily almost choked over her drink. Kate gave her a curious look. "Don't you think so? I assumed that your mate would also be well-endowed, but I suppose that physical size could be deceptive. Why are you laughing?"

"I promise you that Leo isn't short in that department," she managed to say when she finally stopped laughing. "I just didn't expect you to start talking about it."

"It's a perfectly valid observation," Kate said a little defensively. "I find the subject of reproduction fascinating."

Lily started to laugh again. "I prefer hands-on experience."

"It is much more satisfying," Kate agreed. "But the fact that we're both happy makes me hope that perhaps Mary is as well."

Marli whimpered, and A'tai appeared at Kate's side immediately.

"Is she all right? What does she want?"

"She's just hungry." Kate pushed the top of her dress to one side, and the baby immediately latched on and began nursing. Lily watched in fascination as one of her small legs separated and a tiny tentacle began kneading Kate's breast.

"Let me know when she is finished, and I will change her," A'tai said sternly.

"Yes, dear." Kate rolled her eyes at Lily, and Lily laughed.

"He's as bossy as Leo. Do you think all alien males are like that?"

"You will never have a chance to find out about other alien males," Leo growled softly into her ear, and she jumped.

"Are you eavesdropping again?"

"You know I have excellent hearing." He lowered his voice even more. "Although I think we will have to have a little discussion about your lack of appreciation."

"What do you mean?"

"'Not short in that department?' Is that the best you can do?"

"Maybe I need a reminder," she said innocently.

His hand dropped down to squeeze her butt. "That's not all you need."

"Would you like me to show you to your room?" Kate asked, and Lily blushed.

"You will do no such thing," A'tai said immediately. "You will feed our child, and then you will rest."

"I know the way," Leo said as he picked her up and started to carry her off the terrace.

"But we were still talking."

"And you can talk more later. Once you have been reminded to show proper appreciation for your mate."

An hour later, Lily sprawled bonelessly across the bed. She had been thoroughly reminded and a lazy feeling of satisfaction hummed through her veins. The windows were open to the ocean breeze, and she could hear the gentle ebb and flow of the waves against the rocks.

"So... I was thinking," she said slowly.

"Oh?" Leo looked up from where he was unpacking. As usual, he had four times as much luggage as she did. She could hear the suspicious note in his voice and hid a grin.

"Kate's baby is very cute, isn't she?"

"Yes, she is."

"I know we agreed to wait a year, but it really seems as if things are under control and I'm not getting any younger and I just thought that maybe..." *God, why is this so hard?*

"Maybe what?" He had his eyes fixed on her face, but she couldn't read his expression.

"Maybe we should go ahead and think about having a baby," she blurted out.

His roar echoed through the room as he turned back to his luggage, rooting through the case and tossing his clothes aside frantically. Why was he so upset? Her heart sank, but maybe it was had been too soon.

"It was just a suggestion. If you don't want to—"

"Not want to?" He stalked back towards her, holding something in one hand.

"What's that?"

"The pill to reverse my fertility. I've been carrying it for the last six months." He popped it in his mouth, swallowed, and grinned triumphantly.

"Why didn't you say anything?"

"I didn't want to rush you. And we have been busy."

"But you do want to have a baby?"

"More than anything." He shoved down his pants, revealing his cock, already erect and throbbing. "Are you ready for me again? I don't think I can go slowly."

"Yes."

The word was hardly out of her mouth before he pounced on her. He kissed her frantically as his hands traveled over her body, groaning into her mouth when he reached the slick heat between her legs. His tail wrapped around her thigh, pulling it open, and then he thrust into her, hard enough to make her see stars.

Despite her excitement, she struggled to adjust to the sudden intrusion as he set a demanding rhythm. But then his thumb stroked across her clit and the burning stretch became a pleasurable fullness. He growled against her neck, his fangs tracing the mate mark over and over as his hips pistoned into hers. All she could do was cling to him until he roared again, and she felt him explode in her as his fangs sank into her neck and his barbs locked them together.

Her own climax swept over her, so intense that her vision turned dark and it took an endless moment before she was aware of being back in his arms. His tongue swept back and forth over the mating mark, soothing but also sending little shudders of pleasure through her. She felt his embedded cock flex in response.

"Would that pill really work that quickly?" she murmured.

He raised his head and grinned down at her. "Perhaps not. But we will just have to keep trying until it does. I love you, Lily."

"I love you too."

And as he bent his head to kiss her, she could only hope that Mary had found the same happiness.

AUTHOR'S NOTE

Thank you so much for reading **Lily and the Lion**! I had so much fun with Lily and her "big kitty" and I hope you enjoyed their story! I realized as I was writing this story that it's probably as close as I'm ever going to get to a billionaire romance - alien style!

Whether you enjoyed the story or not, it would mean the world to me if you left an honest review on Amazon – reviews are one of the best ways to help other readers find my books!

As always, I have to thank my readers for joining me on these adventures! Your support and encouragement make it possible for me to keep writing these books.

And, as always, a special thanks to my beta team – Janet S, Nancy V, and Kitty S. Your thoughts and comments are incredibly helpful!

Mary's story is next, and this time both the hero and heroine will be on the run! Coming up in - **Mary and the Minotaur**!

AUTHOR'S NOTE

A grumpy, secretive alien. A sweet, not-as-naive-as-she-seems human. A nefarious plot.

Mary and the Minotaur is available on Amazon!

To make sure you don't miss out on any new releases, please visit my website and sign up for my newsletter!

www.honeyphillips.com

OTHER TITLES

The Alien Abduction Series

Anna and the Alien

Beth and the Barbarian

Cam and the Conqueror

Deb and the Demon

Ella and the Emperor

Faith and the Fighter

Greta and the Gargoyle

Hanna and the Hitman

Izzie and the Icebeast

Joan and the Juggernaut

Kate and the Kraken

Lily and the Lion

Mary and the Minotaur

The Alien Invasion Series

Alien Selection

Alien Conquest

Alien Prisoner

Alien Breeder

Alien Alliance

Alien Hope

Exposed to the Elements

The Naked Alien

The Bare Essentials

A Nude Attitude

The Buff Beast

The Strip Down

Cyborgs on Mars

High Plains Cyborg

The Good, the Bad, and the Cyborg

A Fistful of Cyborg

A Few Cyborgs More

The Magnificent Cyborg

The Outlaw Cyborg

Treasured by the Alien

with Bex McLynn

Mama and the Alien Warrior

A Son for the Alien Warrior

Daughter of the Alien Warrior

A Family for the Alien Warrior

The Nanny and the Alien Warrior

Standalone Books

Jackie and the Giant - A Cosmic Fairy Tale

Krampus and the Crone - An SFR Holiday Tale

Anthologies

Alien Embrace

Pets in Space 6

ABOUT THE AUTHOR

Honey Phillips writes steamy science fiction stories about hot alien warriors and the human women they can't resist. From abductions to invasions, the ride might be rough, but the end always satisfies.

Honey wrote and illustrated her first book at the tender age of five. Her writing has improved since then. Her drawing skills, unfortunately, have not. She loves writing, reading, traveling, cooking, and drinking champagne - not necessarily in that order.

Honey loves to hear from her wonderful readers! You can stalk her on her website at www.honeyphillips.com

Or at any of the following locations...

amazon.com/author/honeyphillips
facebook.com/honeyphillipsauthor
instagram.com/honeyphillipsauthor
bookbub.com/authors/honey-phillips

Manufactured by Amazon.ca
Bolton, ON